Max
and
McKenzie

Jeff & Jacqi Lovell

A Mouse Gate™ Adventure

Mouse Gate Press
1103 Middlecreek
Friendswood, Texas 77546
281-992-3131 TEL
www.totalrecallpress.com

Library of Congress Control Number: 2016951298

Printed in the United States of America with simultaneous printings in Australia, Canada, and United Kingdom.

FIRST EDITION
1   2   3   4   5   6   7   8   9   10

To our grandchildren: Noah, Macey, Danny, Luke, Max, Ella, and, McKenzie. What an absolute delight to be able to witness their first trip to Disney World where dreams come alive and ideas are ignited and allowed to bloom. Their enthusiasm is a continual inspiration for us.

Award Winning Authors

Jeff and Jacqi Lovell are both former school teachers and natives of Chicago. Both have graduate degrees from the University of Illinois and Jeff's doctorate is from Vanderbuilt University. Jeff taught high school writing, drama, and literature, and acted as the drama program director for many years. Since retiring, he has also served as a theatre and film critic for a local TV station, and authored several adult adventure/fantasy novels. Over the years Jacqi has taught 4th through 8th grade, specializing in the field of language arts and writing. She has also taught and facilitated bible studies, parent education classes, and LaMaze Childbirth classes.

Introduction

Our Mouse Gate books are designed to expand the imagination and knowledge of young adults between the ages of 8-18 years of age using the medium of adventure and fantasy. The adventures always revolve around their vacation time at Disney World and include time travel where they gain confidence and courage through heroic experiences. In Max and McKenzie, the twins are selected to aid in the discovery of the Lost Ark of the Covenant, but in order to fully understand their assignment they must first participate in a few harrowing experiences that take them back to ancient Israel.

Does the ancient Ark of the Covenant as recorded in biblical history still exist, or is it just a myth? If it does, what has become of it? Could it possibly be discovered today and it's' treasures recovered? The answers to these questions are what the teen-aged twins, Max and McKenzie, are about to discover. During their dream vacation in Walt Disney World, they are transported several times to ancient Israel allowing them to witness the theft of the Ark, become a part of the army that marches around the city of Jericho, watch as the treasures of Solomon's temple are removed, and observe other remarkable events from the past. Included in one of their time travel experiences is an opportunity to participate in an archeological dig unlike any other known to history. How will these discoveries affect them, and possibly, future events?

CHAPTER 1

Well, it was finally here. The day he dreaded all summer had arrived. The first day of his high school career had officially started today and Max was definitely not excited for it to begin. He was very self-conscious about his stuttering problem that would present itself at the worst and most embarrassing moments. He felt he really had no qualities that made him appealing to the other kids, and he hated change. In grade school he'd been accepted because he'd known everyone almost his whole life, many from kindergarten, but now his stomach churned at the thought of having to meet and get to know a whole new group of kids.

Being accepted didn't mean that he had *real* friends, even from his old school. How would he ever make friends here? He resented the kids who were — he hated the word — *popular*. His twin sister McKenzie seemed to be everything he wasn't; *she* was popular, a fine athlete, got terrific grades, and seemed to have boys fawning over her. Max found himself wishing he could be like her, but when he'd mentioned this to her a few days ago, she groaned.

"I wish I didn't have that 'popular' business hanging over my head," she told him. "To tell you the truth, I can't stand most of those kids. They're a big bunch of snobs. A couple of the boys are bullies, downright cruel to others. I don't like that at all. You want to be like them? Good luck."

"B-b-but..." Max began, now flustered at his sister's outburst. His twin sister interrupted.

"But you have a lot going for you," she insisted. "For one thing you're a very good student and a fine artist. You *could* be a terrific athlete, too. Okay, you probably aren't going to be a sprinter on the track team, but so what? Learn how to do shot put, play tennis, or something else. You have to get past this idea that people won't like you just because you have a speech problem once in awhile. Are you going to allow that to ruin your life? Oh, and by the way, you are pretty good looking, too." Then she marched off in a huff. A half block later she stopped, turned, and waited for him to catch up.

Max did not reply, but Kenzie knew he was deep in thought. She felt bad for her twin brother but when he got into a funk over his life, she just felt she needed to shock him out of his self-pity mentality. If he could only see himself as she did. He was good looking with his sandy hair and blue green eyes. She also wished she had been lucky enough to have those long, dark eyelashes. What a waste on a boy! He wasn't very tall, but that would probably change as he got older. And he was smart. He just needed to believe in himself.

The two of them had been walking home from the freshman orientation day at the high school together, and they turned onto their street. They saw their sister, Gina, climbing out of her car with her husband. She had graduated from the Iowa State University of College of Veterinary Medicine, and now she worked at a Veterinary Medical clinic. The twins were excited to see that Colby, her husband, had come with her. Their brother-in-law was a guy both twins adored. They waved at the twins and entered the house.

But the twins had only finished eighth grade. About four long years to go just to finish high school. Max groaned inwardly thinking about it, but dared not say anything aloud then.

Later on, Max did voice his wish that high school was behind them. "What do you think will happen then?" exclaimed his sister when he mentioned it to her. "Is there going to be a magic flash of light, and then your life is suddenly going to get better?"

That shut Max up for a few moments. He hadn't considered that. She was right. When he graduated, he was still going to be him. He wasn't going to change into something better, something stronger, smarter, braver. He was still going to be Max for the rest of his life.

To be sure Max and Kenzie had often discussed the group of kids who did next to nothing at school. They'd go to school, do the bare minimum in class, and get by with Cs and Ds. Their ideal target grade was, in fact, a D-minus, which meant that they hadn't exerted themselves much beyond just showing up.

"I don't know what they could be thinking," said his sister. "What is their life going to be like? They're going to achieve the bare minimum in everything, just like with their effort in school? That is not how I want to live!"

"I don't kn-n-now what to do. I d-d-d-don't want to be like that," Max stuttered, aware that his shyness could allow him to avoid activities as well as trying to make friends with others.

"Well, take charge of it!" she challenged, in a quarrelsome voice. "You love football. Go and see the Coach; go out for the team and start practicing!" He knew that voice. He'd heard her use it all her life when she was spoiling for a fight. But he didn't want to fight.

"I d-d-d-don't know," he said. "It might be a little late to try out for football. I should have been working out with the team already. I'd be c-c-c-coming in a few days behind."

"Well, you will never know if you don't try, will you!" his sister bellowed again. "Look, last year all you did was come home after school and eat chips and fritos and drink soda, and then sit and play those stupid video games. You can do better! Go out for football and get involved!"

Max didn't much like the idea of going to football practice unprepared. When he and his sister walked into their house, he found that his older sister, Gina, and her husband, Colby, were already visiting with Mom and Dad.

"Hey, Colby," Max said. "Want to play some catch?"

McKenzie noticed that Max didn't stutter when he was with Colby. Max felt accepted and safe with Colby. He was patient and kind, and always willing to spend time with Max. If only he could come to that point with the other kids, she thought.

Colby perked up. "Sure, Buddy," he said, using the nickname he had affectionately assigned to Max when he met him years ago. Max found his football, changed into some sweats and jogged out to the backyard with Colby.

Colby had been all-state in football as a high school senior, as well as Special Mention all-state as a junior, and he knew the game well. He planned to coach at the high school this year. All summer he had coached Max in how to throw the ball correctly, how to play the position of quarterback, and Max fell into it quickly. His brother-in-law was pleased with how well Max listened and completed his passes. "Hey, Buddy, you are doing great. You need to go out for football this year before it's too late."

Max frowned, not convinced his abilities were up to the task.

But Colby picked up on that right away. "I'm serious, Max, you're a natural," he said. "You just need some confidence and to believe in yourself." Colby ruffled Max's hair and patted him on the back.

So, before school the next morning, Max, feeling a desperate nervousness, summoned the courage to walk into Coach Colbrese's office. He was the head football coach, but Max didn't know what to do other than talk to him.

The coach greeted him and Max introduced himself. Coach shook hands with him and he worried that Coach noticed how nervous he was and how sweaty his hands were. But the coach just grinned at him, attempting to put him at ease.

"Can I help you, Son?" asked the coach.

Max took a deep breath. "Yeah, I m-m-m-mean, yessir."

The coach grinned. "Okay," said Colbrese. "What's up?"

"Mr. Colbrese, I know I sh-sh-should have started a few days ago," fumbled Max, now willing himself not to stutter. He told himself to speak slowly. "But I'd like to c-c-come out for football."

"How about tonight?" asked Coach.

"Oh!" said Max. "Well, if th-that's okay…"

"You're a freshman, right?" asked Coach.

"Yessir," said Max.

"Can you meet me by the freshman locker room right after school?" asked Coach.

"Yessir," agreed Max. The coach offered his hand and Max shook it, giving the coach the best grip he could muster. And so it was concluded. Max was so excited he had to restrain himself from giving the coach a 'high five'. He shuffled out of the office with a smile on his face.

He met his twin sister as they started into the lunchroom. "I did it," he announced as soon as he spotted her. "I talked to the coach."

"Hey, that's great," she smiled. "I'm proud of you. When do you start?"

"Tonight," he said. "I won't be able to play for a few weeks, but that's okay. I have to get into sh-sh-shape, y'know."

She laughed and punched his arm.

CHAPTER 2

The equipment manager, a good natured man named Pop Fligh, helped Max get his practice uniform on and adjust the pads. Then, Pop assigned him a locker, gave him a key for the locker, told him not to lose it, and gave Max a little push towards the door to the practice field.

When Max arrived at the field, he found the team throwing the ball around and loosening up. The varsity was using the first practice field, about a hundred yards away. The sophomore team occupied the second field, and he saw the freshman team on a third field about two hundred yards away.

Max began to trot, aware of the weight of the equipment he had on. He was nervous and scared. He was beginning to feel a little nauseated and wanted to turn around and go in, change clothes, and never think about football again.

A voice next to him said, "No. You've come this far. You can do it." Max turned to look, but no one stood there. He pivoted all the way around, but he was all alone.

Great, he thought. I'm not scared enough, I guess. Now I'm hearing voices.

Reaching the freshman field, he saw a man standing and watching. "Excuse me, Sir," he said.

The man turned and looked at him.

"Yes, Son?"

"I'm Max Rizza," he said. "I'm just c-c-c-coming out for the team."

"Here," said the man, and flipped him a football. "Throw it."

Max calmed himself and ran through what Colby had taught him. He spread his fingers over the football's laces. He felt awkward as he drew back his arm and threw the ball to a boy about twenty yards away.

To his mild surprise, the ball sailed straight to the boy in a tight spiral, just as Colby had shown him. "Good," said the coach. The other boy threw the ball back, but it wobbled quite a bit. Again Max threw a tight spiral back.

Max stared at the ball, the arc it created in the air still imprinted on his brain. It had gone on a straight line, the nose of the ball tilting down as it reached the other player. He had thrown it exactly as Colby had been teaching him.

Max grinned. A bit of the nervousness ebbed away and he felt better.

"You throw a good ball," said the man. "I'm Coach Morinec."

"Yessir," replied Max, blushing at the compliment, and thankful for all of Colby's patient instruction. "My name is Max Rizza."

"You wouldn't be Gina's brother, would you?" asked the coach.

"Yessir, I am," nodded Max. "You know her?"

"Yeah, yeah," said Coach. "One of my favorite kids ever. You've got quite a bit to live up to, Son."

"Yessir," grinned Max.

"I think I heard she'd married Colby, is that right?" added the coach.

Max nodded. Coach whacked him on the shoulder. "Another great kid," he announced. Again Max nodded. "We'll talk after calisthenics," said Coach Morinec.

He put a whistle to his mouth and blew it. The rest of the team fell into four lines of about 10 to 15 guys each. Coach yelled at one of the boys. "Howard," he said. "Lead cals tonight."

"Yessir," said a tall, skinny boy. He stepped in front of the group and yelled, "Jumping Jacks. Ready?" The team yelled in unison, "Go!"

Fifty jumping jacks later, Howard yelled for pushups, and the team did twenty. Then they did sit-ups, something called burpees, stretching, and other calisthenics that never seemed to end.

Max had begun to conclude that he was going to pass out. Once the exercises were completed, Max stumbled for a few moments, dizzy and nauseated. Coach called him over.

"Good effort in cals," said Coach Morinec. "It'll get better. Come on over here with the quarterbacks."

Max, staggering a little, resolved to get it together. He took a couple of deep breaths, a long drink of water, and broke into a light jog over to the quarterback area. The dizziness vanished in a few seconds and he felt better. For the next several minutes one of the coaches taught him and two other boys how to play the position. Max had a little catching up to do, but he proved to be a quick learner.

The quarterbacks worked on the basics of the positions, and spent several moments throwing the ball to one another.

After an hour, Coach Morinec blew his whistle. The players ran into the center of the practice field and participated in tackling and blocking drills for some time.

At last, practice ended and the weary players trooped

toward the locker room. Max jumped into a quick shower, dressed and started to walk home. Two or three of the other freshman players stopped him on the sidewalk in front of the school. "Hey, Max, you heading our way?" one of them asked, and Max nodded. "We're stopping for a quick soda at Mark's house. You free to come?"

"S-s-sure," Max responded. As the afternoon went on Max wondered if maybe this was going to be a way to make new friends. (To himself, he thought, please help me not to stutter again). At moments like this he always wished he was more like his extroverted twin sister. But these guys laughed with him, joked with him, teased him, and genuinely seemed to like being with him. No one even mentioned his stutter, which amazed him. Maybe, he thought, just maybe, this football thing would be the best decision he had made in a long time and in more than one way.

The group left Mark's house, each going their separate ways. Walking home, Max thought about the fun he had at Mark's with the other guys. He decided he really was glad McKenzie pushed him to go out for football, despite the rigorous practice sessions that were involved. Maybe he really would be able become part of a group of friends. The thought brightened his spirits and gave him a little more confidence.

He turned the corner and saw a tall, slim man standing in the parkway in front of his parents' house, but Max didn't pay much attention until the man spoke to him.

"Hello, Max," the man said.

Max was so surprised he couldn't respond at first. "Hello," he managed, wondering how this man knew him.

"We haven't met before," said the Man, smiling. "However,

I do know you. I have watched you for many years now."

"M-m-m-me?" said Max, feeling rather silly at his lack of speaking ability, and perhaps a little nervous at the thought of a stranger watching him over a lengthy period of time. The Man stepped forward and put his hands on Max' head. Max felt a warm, pleasant glow spread over him. All of his exhaustion and fear dropped away at the man's gentle touch.

In a few moments, the man put his hand on Max' shoulder and smiled at him. "I came because I wanted to tell you a few things," said the man. "First, we are proud of you."

Max again found himself without words, just staring at the man with a quizzical look.

"Yes, we are," continued the Man. "It took some courage to start to play football. We take great pleasure in courage. Second, I will come to see you often. We have something we'll want you to do. Please call me Curiel."

"Yes, S-s-s-sir," muttered Max.

"Third: Do you still have your amulet?"

Max took a step backwards. Now he was perplexed. How did this man know about the amulet? A friend of their sister named Marina, and her husband Dan, had given each of the twins an amulet, which looked like circular golden crystals on golden chains. Marina and Dan were stern in their advice not to lose them. Dan had explained that one day the twins would understand their importance and what they could be used for.

Max had been very careful with his. "Yes, Sir," Max replied, a little nervous. "I k-k-k-keep it in the drawer next to my bed."

"That is wise," said the man. "You will need it soon. Be sure that you and McKenzie take them with you when you go on the trip."

Then the Man vanished. There was no sound effect, no flashing lights or smoke, no wind or storm. One moment he stood talking to Max. Then, he was gone. *What in the world does that mean?* thought Max. *I am not going anywhere, and who was that guy?*

CHAPTER 3

Max stood on the sidewalk, stunned and speechless for several moments until a car pulled up in front of the house and parked. Gina and Colby stepped out of the car.

"Hi, li'l bro," greeted Gina.

"Hey, Max, what's up?" said Colby.

Max turned and stared at his sister. Her expression turned to one of concern. "What's the matter with you, Max?" she asked, giving him a hug around his shoulders. "You look like you have seen a ghost."

Max shook off his surprise. "Hi, Gina, hi, Colby," he managed. "Maybe I did. I j-j-j-just had something strange happen to me." He sketched out the meeting with the Man named Curiel.

Both Gina and Colby listened carefully as he related the story. By the time Max finished explaining his encounter with the stranger they were both nodding their heads and smiling at him.

Max was confused by their reaction, "Don't you guys think that was pretty weird?" he asked.

"Was his name was Curiel?" asked Gina, and Max nodded. "We have met Him, Max," she confided. "You don't need to be worried or concerned. Our adventures were always with the Angel named Curiel."

"An Angel," said Max, allowing his voice to reflect his unbelief. "R-r-right."

"I'm not making it up," insisted his sister.

Colby agreed. "Look, every once in a while things happen we can't explain in logical terms. Tell me: did you feel afraid when you were talking to this person?"

Max thought. "Well, y-y-yes," he said. "At first. Then He calmed me down. I wasn't afraid once he began to talk."

"Right," said Colby. "Did he put his hands on your head?"

Again Max considered the question. "Yeah," he shrugged. "As soon as he did that, I didn't feel afraid at all. In fact, I had the feeling I'd never be afraid again."

"Uh, huh," said Gina. "Let me change the subject, okay? Did you try out for football tonight?"

"Yeah," he said. "It isn't really a matter of trying out. Anyone who shows up makes the team. You have to quit to get off the team."

"Right," said Colby. "I remember when I went through freshman football. The first couple of weeks were awful. You feel like you're going to die, but then you don't, then you think you're going to quit, and then you decide you won't, and so on."

"He wound up loving it," said Gina, taking Colby's arm. "He didn't quit."

Max knew what she was saying. Gina knew that he really looked up to Colby, respected him, and saw him as a role model. "I'm not qu-qu-quitting," he said, hoping he sounded resolute. He didn't want his sister and her husband to see that he was afraid. And he especially did not want Colby to think of him as a quitter. Football challenged him. He wasn't sure he was up to it. But he really hoped he could hang in there.

"I know," said Colby, responding as if he could read what

going through Max's mind. "I wasn't sure either when I first went out."

How does he know what I am thinking! thought Max. How did he manage that? He started to say, "Well, I'm not sure I'm afraid…"

"Yes, you are, Max," said his sister. "Anything that scares us does so because we don't think we're good enough. Everyone has a fear they might fail and look stupid. Don't you sense that?"

Max nodded, but he wasn't sure everyone had that fear. He was having a hard time talking. "Remember the magazine and TV ad?" said Colby. "'Just do it!!!'"

"Okay, I'll t-t-try…" murmured Max.

"No," said Colby. "Don't try. Do it. Do it to the best of your ability."

Now his older sister took his arm. She gave him an encouraging smile. A pleasant series of memories ran through his mind. His sister teaching him to ride a bike. Babysitting him and his twin sister. Fixing them macaroni and cheese, and peanut butter and jelly sandwiches. One night when their parents were out for the evening, she was babysitting the twins and he got scared. How old was he? Four, maybe five. He woke up screaming and crying with a nightmare.

But Gina had come into his room and sat next to him. She comforted him, sang to him, and calmed him down in a few moments.

She has always been wonderful to him. He'd never thought about it much, but he really did have a terrific big sister: loyal, kind, and good. She had this wonderful compassion for others, and an instinctive love for animals. When she worked with the animals at her practice, they grew calm, relaxed and unafraid.

Once when he had been helping her at her practice he watched her put down a sweet dog only about a year old. The little dog was beautiful, but had been desperately sick his whole life, and she had never thrived. Max thought he might throw up as he watched his sister ease the little animal out of this life, but no, he felt no terror, no anger, no dismay of any kind.

Then Gina went to work with the little dog's owners, who had come to love the puppy. The dog had been born and raised in a puppy mill where breeders only cared about making money with little concern for the health of the animal. The couple had brought the puppy in many times already with multiple health problems.

As Gina put the dog to sleep, both husband and wife were crying, and she comforted them. She talked about how they were right to choose the euthanasia option: this dog never had a chance of being healthy, would never be happy, and they would have ruinous vet bills. She said that she knew they couldn't think about all this now, but in a day or two they'd feel better.

Max remembered watching his sister, admiring her poise, her confidence and her gentle nature. She took the couple to her office and sat with them, being gentle and kind as the husband and his wife grieved. Gina advised the couple to find another dog as soon as possible.

"Do you have a suggestion?" asked the husband.

"Glad you asked," Gina said with a smile. "Yes, I do. We have a nice dog, a four year old mixed breed, that an owner just brought in. The woman cried about having to give up the dog, but her children developed allergies, and the family couldn't keep her. They didn't want to put her down, because she is such a nice little thing and quite healthy." The husband and wife exchanged glances and nodded, and the wife asked if they could see her. Gina sent Max to get the dog.

Max walked back into the kennel. He took a leash from the wall and hooked up the dog, whose name was Zoey. The dog, calm and gentle, rubbed against him as they walked down the hall. He leaned down and petted her.

The husband and wife looked up with a bit of apprehension at Zoey. "She *is* a pretty little thing, isn't she," said the husband, after a few seconds.

"Yes," said Gina, as the dog, wagging her tail enthusiastically, came over to let the couple pet her.

"What breed is she?" asked the wife. The wife wiped her tears with a tissue, and the husband took a drink from a bottle of water Gina had given him.

Gina grinned, and now both husband and wife smiled with her. "Heaven knows," said Gina. "She's got some shepherd, some poodle, probably a little lab. We could run a swab and test her DNA if it is truly important to you. The point is, she's a very healthy and gentle dog." Max also smiled, watching his sister work with the people, who were rising above their sadness and falling in love with the sweet little animal.

Ten minutes later, the people left with Zoey. Gina let out a whoop and gave her brother a little punch on the arm as they watched the grieving couple, devastated by the loss of their puppy, walk to their car in the parking lot. Though they would grieve about the little dog for a few weeks, even months, they left the parking lot smiling with a healthy, well-mannered dog that would bring them years of joy. "Nice job, Max," she said, giving him a high five.

"Me?" he blinked, surprised by the compliment. "I didn't do anything."

"Yes you did," his sister insisted. "They saw how well Zoey related to you, and that gave them confidence."

"Thanks, Sis," said Max. He appreciated what she said. "How do you do it?" he asked. "I mean, how do you put animals to sleep? Isn't it hard?"

Gina put an arm around him. "I know what you mean," she said softly. "It's the worst part of my job. But, like in this case, when I have to do it, it's almost always the right and necessary thing to do."

"What do you mean?"

"For example," said Gina. "We had a dog brought in a few weeks ago. He was a nice looking dog, healthy, but unpredictable. He went after their little boy and bit him on the cheek while the boy was setting his food down on the floor. I talked to the owners about it. They finally decided to put the dog down."

"They'd tried everything?" asked Max.

"I don't know what else they could have done," she nodded. "They even hired a trainer. The dog was abused as a puppy, not trained properly, and formed irreversible habits. The owners gave the dog another chance but when he went after their baby crawling on the floor, they decided it was the best thing. They didn't want another family to have something tragic happen to their child or the dog to be abused, so they decided to start over with a dog that they could live with, do you see? They had been lied to when they first got him. The man told them he was only about two years old and it was later they found out the truth, that this dog had a history of violent behavior."

Max shrugged away the memory as Gina walked with him into the house, her arm through his. Max, with a start, realized that he felt proud to have Gina as his sister and Colby as his brother-in-law. Very proud.

Gina, almost six feet tall, had classic Italian good looks. She wore her auburn hair long, down past her shoulders and her face glowed with intelligence, kindness, and grace.

Her husband Colby stood about 6'-5", and he had a solid build like a linebacker. His blond hair was cut short, and he seemed to be always smiling or laughing.

Gina led her brother through the door, followed by Colby, and they began to joke with him and put him at ease.

I guess Gina has what they call a gift, he thought: a gift of compassion, kindness, and confidence. She was going to be a great veterinarian and a great mom.

CHAPTER 4

Dinner that night was a typical family night with everyone gathered around the table sharing Mom's old fashioned pot roast with carrots, potatoes, and lots of Mom's yummy gravy....everyone's favorite comfort food meal. Mom usually went all out to please with the menu when Colby and Gina joined them for dinner. As always, there was lots of conversation, laughter, and good-natured teasing.

Football tomorrow, Max asserted to himself. I won't be afraid. I will not be nervous. I'll be okay.

* * * * *

Mom had to shake McKenzie the next morning to wake her up. The teenager managed to drag herself out of bed and started her morning exercise routine. It only took about ten minutes, but it did serve to wake her up.

She set a stopwatch alarm and began to run in place. First, she extended her arms behind her and stretched them upwards, counting to 15. Then she completed her arm stretches until the timer for the four minute routine went off. Then she bent forward from the waist placing her hands flat on the floor stretching out her Achilles tendon. She finished her routine with thirty-five pushups, 50 abdominal crunchers, and another general stretch.

Her sister Gina had shown her that routine and she'd done it four or five times a week for the last few years. When she finished, she breathed deep to force oxygen into her lungs, through her heart and to her muscles.

She grinned as she thought about her friends at school, who hated P.E. class. She found it easier not to talk about it with them since she loved the break from all her classes. Also she liked how she felt after her morning exercises. She was more alert and cheerful, and she noticed that she slept better at night when she did this routine in the morning.

McKenzie jumped into a shower, towel dried her hair, and then brushed it out. Like her brother, she had curly hair, more blond than sandy colored. She wished looked more like her sister. She loved Gina's lovely auburn hair and felt a little envious of her older sister: finished with school, married, into a good career, and above all, happy. McKenzie shrugged the jealousy away.

Her friends considered McKenzie fun to be around, and for the most part pretty happy, but she wasn't happy today. She and her twin brother had been at odds for some time. He'd been going through some major changes as he matured, and he'd have times when he was surly and even unkind. McKenzie had of course been experiencing physical changes also, but she hadn't disliked or resented it. Exercise and athletics at school had helped her to maintain a positive attitude.

McKenzie dressed in jeans, a shirt in her school's colors and some sandals. She bolted downstairs and found her parents and her brother talking about their plans for the day. She was pleased and surprised to find her sister Gina walking in through the garage door and into the kitchen with Colby where they joined the family at the breakfast table.

McKenzie blurted, "What're you doing here?" as if her

sister's presence in the kitchen was about as unexpected as a helicopter landing on the front porch. At once she realized how that sounded and apologized. "I mean, I'm glad you're here but you guys never come for breakfast during the week."

Gina wasn't offended and laughed, "Well, we came to make you an offer I don't think you'll want to refuse. We haven't told Max, either, but it concerns him as well. Also, maybe Mom and Dad."

Colby's eyes were sparkling and he wore a silly smile on his face, at the same time producing a thumbs up gesture. "What she means is, we're going to do something really fun, and we want you guys to join us," pointing at Max and McKenzie.

McKenzie's mouth dropped open just a little. "What do you mean?" she questioned.

Gina, a smirk on her face, looked busy as she buttered a piece of toast, and she put a bit of scrambled egg on the bread. Her husband duplicated her movements. Gina placed it in her mouth and slowly chewed, clearly enjoying dragging out this moment, all the while staring at her sister.

"Gina!" scolded Mom, when the silence had lengthened a bit. "It's not nice to tease your brother and sister."

Gina and Colby both laughed. "Okay," she agreed. "How would you two feel about a week in Disney World later this fall?"

The twins stared at their sister, again stunned. "D-d-d-disney?" blurted Max.

"You mean in Florida?" asked McKenzie.

"Yep," said Colby and Gina in unison.

"When?" asked Max, trying to curb his growing excitement.

"Does that mean you'd be interested?" asked his older sister.

"Of course we would!" screeched McKenzie, speaking for both of them. Her sister and brother-in-law laughed.

"It's like this," said Gina. "I have a conference in Disney the week just before the week of Thanksgiving. "Dr. Roberts, you know, the man who owns the vet practice?"

"Yes," said the twins.

"Well, he *was* going to go," shrugged Gina. "But his wife has become sick, and she won't be able to travel for quite a while. I don't believe it is too serious, but she's uncomfortable and likely to have to do a couple months of high-power antibiotics."

"And it just so happens there is an coaches' conference for new coaches in Orlando I would like to attend during the same time period," added Colby.

"Anyhow," continued Gina, "the conference begins on a Monday and ends at noon on Friday. The meetings last all day, but we'll have breakfast and dinner together every day. I've secured reservations for one night at the Whispering Canyon Cafe in the Wilderness Lodge. A couple of my friends thought it would be a lot of fun and recommended we eat there. Other than meals, you two are going to be on your own in the parks. I'd like to go Saturday to Saturday, leaving at 6:00 A. M. on Saturday and coming back on the following Saturday at about 9:00 P. M. I am assuming that since you guys are pretty good students you could miss a couple days of school."

"I don't know how we could pay for it," mumbled Max. "I don't have much money saved."

"Me neither," moaned McKenzie.

"Aha," said their sister. "For me, that's a highlight of the trip. I'll let you earn it. I'm willing to hire you for weekends at my practice: cleaning up, caring and feeding for the animals, and so on. I think it is a win/win situation for all of us. Well, what do you think?"

The twins really had nothing to think about. Kenzie and Max jumped at the opportunity to go to their favorite place in the world. So it was settled. Max and McKenzie agreed to begin working at their sister's business and were able to arrange a work schedule around their commitments. Even though they found themselves working harder than they had anticipated, they enjoyed being around the animals and their sister. Gina proved to be a tireless teacher and taught them all she could about veterinary medicine.

They weren't expecting to be paid much, but their sister paid them the same wage any other help would have earned, allowing them an ample amount of spending money for their upcoming trip.

CHAPTER 5

The first freshman football game came about two weeks later. Max didn't feel too nervous, because the games were played on Saturday morning and the crowds weren't big, just parents and coaches for the most part.

Max began tugging on his uniform about forty-five minutes before the game started. He plopped down on one of the benches in the locker room. When Max looked up, he realized varsity coach Colbrese had walked over and he sat down next to him.

"How are you doing, Max?" Coach asked him. Coach Morinec then came over and stood in front of him.

"I feel okay, Coach," Max said. "I hope I get to p-p-play." *Darn!* he thought. *What a lousy time to stutter!*

"You'll do more than that," said Coach Morinec. "You're starting at quarterback. Get out there and loosen up."

Max felt as though an entire family of monarch butterflies had suddenly taken up residence in his stomach. He finished adjusting his uniform, grabbed his helmet and hustled from the locker room out to the Field.

Oh boy, thought Max. *I didn't think I'd start. Yow.* The nervousness grew, and he hoped he could live up to the confidence Coach had placed in him. *What if I bomb out?* Negative thoughts swirled around in his head. He had to shake it off. He could do this. *Calm down and focus*, he told himself.

Max went out and threw thirty or more passes to loosen up

his arm. His stomach didn't seem to want to relax. He worked harder than usual at calisthenics and stretching, hoping his gut would settle down.

Time zoomed by and soon the other team kicked off. Max's friend Jerry Reacher took the ball and returned it to about the 35 yard line. The kickoff team came off the field and Jerry swatted his buddy's shoulder pads in encouragement.

"You okay, Max?" asked Coach Morinec.

"Y-y-yesir," lied Max, hoping he looked confident.

"Right," said Coach Morinec. "Look, the old Chicago Cardinals, who've since moved to St. Louis and then to Phoenix, had a great quarterback named Paul Crisman. My dad got to meet him once. He said that Paul told him a story. Paul said he would feel kind of yucky with nerves until the first time he'd get tackled in the game. Then he'd be okay."

"Yeah, I guess that m-m-m-makes sense," nodded Max.

"Okay," said Coach Morinec, his hand on Max's shoulder pads. "Then let's start with that quarterback keeper and I'll send you another play. Hold onto that ball!"

The other team kicked off to Max's team. Max's friend, Tim DeRosa, caught the ball and ran it back to about the thirty yard line where he got tackled.

Max buckled his chin strap and ran onto the field and joined the huddle. "Come on, Max," said Tim, the fullback. "Get us going." Max knelt down in the huddle, took a deep breath, and called the play. He noticed he was able to call it without stuttering.

Max took the ball from Chris Mackie, the center, and faked a handoff to Tim, who plunged into the line and got hit by about 30 guys, it seemed. Max tucked the ball onto his hip and rolled out to his left, looking as if he was just ducking away from the line of scrimmage.

The action surged past him, no one paying attention to him. Max looked up the field. To his shock, it was wide open.

Max tucked the ball into his gut, holding on with both hands. He ran past the line of scrimmage and reached full speed in two more steps. He heard the crowd screaming and heard Coach Morinec yelling encouragement. 10 yards. Then 20. He heard a player coming up behind him and he turned on the jets, running as fast as he could.

He felt someone grab at his uniform, but he ducked right and the hand loosened. Now he'd gained thirty yards. Forty. Another player grabbed his uniform jersey, and he twisted and the hand let go. Ten yards to the end zone! He thought at the beginning of the run that he was charging as fast as he could. Then, when he heard the tacklers bearing down on him, he tightened his grip on the ball and found *another* gear, going even faster. There's a difference, he thought, between actually *doing* your best and *thinking* you're doing your best.

Suddenly he felt two defenders smack him and he went down hard. He started to get to his feet. As he did so, he became aware of his team's parent group cheering, and his teammates yelling. He was gasping for breath. His hearing cleared up as his teammates surged up and pulled him to his feet, all of them jumping in excitement. They began dragging him back to the sidelines, pummeling him on the back and yelling their appreciation of the—**Touchdown**?

Now his accomplishment registered. "I scored a touchdown," he murmured to himself, but Coach Morinec had put his arm around him and heard what he said.

"You sure did," affirmed Coach Morinec, giving him a hug. "That's a pretty good start to your football career. Do you think you can do it again?"

Max shrugged. His stomach didn't hurt. "Give me the ball," he said, his grin spreading over the width of his face.

And he didn't stutter!

CHAPTER 6

With Max at quarterback the freshman team won six games and lost two. Over the last couple weeks of the season Max began to realize that he'd made several good friends: guys who ate lunch with him, walked home with him, and kept in touch through text messages.

The freshman football season ended the last week of October, though the Varsity played on for three more games. In the state tournament, Varsity lost to the team that went on to win the state championship, and the school and its community was enthusiastic about how well the school's football program had done.

Max was walking to school one day with his sister and felt grateful to her. Deep down he knew that he owed her a big thank you. "Look, Kenz, I need to apologize."

His sister gave him a wry smile. "Apologize for what?" she asked.

"I've had a great time in football," he continued, "and I guess I owe a lot of it to you. You're the one who yelled at me to get my butt in gear. I was sitting around feeling sorry for myself and being lazy. At first I resented what you said but this was one of the best decisions I ever made, and now, for the first time, I even have some great friends."

"My gym teacher talked to me about that," she said. "She likes my attitude in P. E., I guess. She told me, 'Look, Kenzie. Life is work. What you should do with your education isn't just pile up grades. Find what it is that gets you out of bed in the morning. Do that.' And that got me thinking about what I was doing."

Max nodded in agreement. It was pretty good advice. Now that he thought about it, he felt better for having admitted he had been wrong, and she'd been right.

When the freshman season ended, Max's buddy, Matt Brewster, walked over and sat down next to him at lunch. He was dragging Kenny Booth and Steve Grant with him; all three of them had played on the football team this past season.

"Look," said Matt. "We think we've got some talent on our team."

"I agree," said Max. "I think we can do pretty well next year."

"What would you think if we would start working out together after school?" suggested Kenny. "Say about an hour or so. We can meet in the field house or a gym or even go outside if we get a nice day and run pass patterns, all that sort of stuff. We ought to sharpen up, don't you think?"

"We went to Coach and asked him what he thought. He suggested that we do it three days a week, and help each other out," added Steve.

"Will he come?" asked Max. "I mean, it'd be good to have him watching."

Steve shook his head. "I don't think he can," he explained. "I think that may violate state rules. But I'll ask again."

"I'll go with you," nodded Max.

That was the beginning of the after school football club. The four boys met three days a week for a few weeks. Then the rest of the team, those who weren't in other sports, like basketball or wrestling or swimming, also started coming. They limited the workouts to about an hour, but they found that the plays, the passing patterns, and all the movements of football were becoming more and more exact and sharp.

One thing Max liked was that the guys on the team helped him out. They critiqued what he did, and he returned the favor. He refused to let the criticism hurt his feelings. He took their criticism as a favor and learned to put aside his natural defensiveness.

Max, by nature rather shy and withdrawn, found that by making firm friends with the other players he had experienced a whole shift in how he viewed himself and others. They greeted each other in the halls and he was included in their social plans. He was becoming more self-confident.

He and McKenzie began getting along better as well. The bickering and arguing had subsided, and they had started helping and encouraging each other more.

"I've been feeling like..." he stammered to his twin sister one evening as they were walking home together. It was the Thursday before Thanksgiving week, and the twins were excited about a few days off from school, but also because they were going to Disney World in a matter of hours.

"Feeling like?" asked his sister.

"Feeling, well, I guess blessed is the right word," explained Max. "Does that sound silly? It's just that I'm feeling really good about everything going on in my life right now."

"Right," encouraged McKenzie. "No, I don't think that sounds silly or strange. Why do you think that is?"

Max thought for a second. "I guess because I've been trying new things, like football, and it has turned out pretty well. I have always been afraid of trying new things. So, anyway, now

I may even decide to go out for wrestling after we get back from Florida."

"I think that's great, bro," said McKenzie. "This change started after you signed up for football, didn't it."

Max considered. "Yeah, that's right," he agreed. "Gina told me that you sometimes just have to step up and do some things that really kind of scare you."

"I know what you mean," she said. "Like when you went in to see Coach Colbrese, right?"

Max hadn't really thought it all through. "I guess so," he reasoned. "When you try something and do okay, it builds up your confidence, don't you think?"

"Even if you don't do okay, at least you've tried it out," noted McKenzie. "Having some success has made you a lot happier, hasn't it?"

"Definitely," he said. "Colby's advice was, 'Just do it. Don't worry about the results.'"

"Gina said that to me, too," said McKenzie. "If you fail at something, at least you've tried it."

"Right," he said.

"And when you're in a situation, you don't want to quit until you've done your best."

"Yeah, for sure," he said.

"We have to pack tonight, you know," announced his sister, changing the subject.

He perked up at that comment. "Okay," he said. "We leave in two wake-ups. Hey, Kenzie, we should wear those amulets that Marina and Dan gave us. Don't forget, o.k.?"

"Gosh, Max, why do we need those? What even made you think of them?"

"I don't know, but I just feel strongly that we need to bring them. Promise me you will." Max wondered if he should tell her about the man, Curiel, that he met that day on the way home from school. He probably should have confided in her when it happened, but he'd been so busy that he'd sort of forgotten about it until this trip. Plus, at that point they had been arguing a lot. Oh, well, he would have plenty off time to fill her in when they got to Disney.

"Sure, Max," Kenzie replied, wondering what that was all about.

CHAPTER 7

At 4:15 A. M. on Saturday, a horn honked outside their front door. Gina and Colby hopped out of the airport taxi and waved, running up to the door and yelling for Max and Kenzie to "Come on!"

The twins were ready and had been watching at the window for the cab. After hurried goodbyes to their parents, they hustled out the door and into the taxi. The driver helped them load their luggage and then sped off to O'Hare Airport.

The drive to O'Hare International Airport only took a half an hour at that time of the morning. Once their bags were checked, the twins soon found themselves on the plane, waiting for takeoff at 6:00 A. M.

"Well, we're on our way," squealed McKenzie, unable to contain her excitement.

"Yep," replied Max, trying to remain cool.

"Look, Max," said McKenzie. "We need to talk about this week and how we're going to behave, you know?"

"What do you mean?"

"We have to be responsible," reasoned McKenzie. "Mom and Dad, our sister and brother-in-law, aren't going to be supervising us at every moment, you know?"

He paused for a second, starting to become annoyed. "So what are you saying? 'We can't have any fun?'"

"No!" she barked. "No, of course not. What I mean is that we have to be considerate. We can't do things that would make

Gina worry about us, or doubt us, or anything like that. We have to let her know what we're doing, where we're going, all that. Did you remember your cell phone?"

"Yeah, of course," he sulked, trying to imagine what horrible things she thought he would do to disappoint their sister. He resented when she tried to lecture him. "I even remembered the charging cable," he added in a sarcastic voice.

"I didn't mean to say it like that," she said. Max knew that she was apologizing, and he shrugged in acceptance of her apology. "When we get there, I keep getting a feeling that we're going to have an great adventure. Don't you feel it?"

He thought about the Angel Curiel again. Maybe this was the time to tell her. Yeah, he felt something was going to happen but could not explain this as it seemed so illogical. Ever since his conversation about Curiel with Colby and Gina he was almost waiting for something to occur, and now that they left for this trip, well, Curiel had been specific about taking the amulets on a trip. So Gina could be right; we could be in for some kind of a major adventure.

The plane landed, and the twins fell in step behind their sister and her husband as they left the terminal.

"Oh my gosh, sunshine and 76*. Isn't this amazing!" shouted Kenzie, and then let out a "Wa-hoo!" Everyone laughed at her enthusiastic arrival in Florida.

They met their limousine driver outside at the arrival terminal. He took charge of the group, helped them with their luggage, and soon the limousine was speeding toward the exotic Polynesian Resort. The beautiful facility was located not far from the Magic Kingdom on the monorail route.

Max had been trying to remain cool while the car made its

way to the Polynesian Resort, but they spotted the famous Mouse Ears on top of the Water Tower in the park. He elbowed his twin and pointed, and they each gave a thumbs up.

"Oh, yes," they shouted in unison.

Their sister turned around from the front seat and asked, "What's up?"

The twins pointed at the Mouse Ears, and the anticipation of the great week they could look forward to made them laugh out loud. Gina grinned, as did her husband Colby. "Yeah," she said. "You guys want some lunch before we head over to a park?"

"Sure," said Max, who was never known to turn down a meal. Besides, they only had a granola bar on the plane and he was now in ravenous mode.

"No, let's go to Epcot!" said his twin sister McKenzie, with equal excitement.

Their sister and her husband laughed, and the discussion continued while they unpacked the luggage. Their rooms were in the Samoa building so they were close to the pool area which was a plus to the twins. Max and Kenzie changed into shorts and tee shirts and ran down to the Kona Cafe restaurant, Gina assuring them that she and her husband would join them in moments.

The Kona Cafe was located on the second floor of the area known as the Great Ceremonial Hall and had a wide breakfast menu. Luckily, they arrived between main mealtimes so only had to wait about 10 minutes for a table. "Okay, what do we want to do?" asked Kenzie, anxious to get the day moving along.

Max, intent on ordering food as quickly as possible, was busy studying the menu. "Uh-huh", mumbled Max.

"Well, we're right next to the Magic Kingdom," continued McKenzie. "Maxwell, are you listening to me?"

"Oh, man, I have to have the Tonga toast. It's banana stuffed French toast with a cinnamon sugar coating. That sounds awesome. Where's the waitress? I'm ready to order. What are you having, Kenz?"

"Oh, let me see. I guess you won't focus on our plans for the day until we order," she grumbled. "Wow, everything really does sound yummy. Hmmm. I think I'll go with the Macadamia Pineapple Pancakes and bacon. O.K., now that that's decided, can we please figure out what to do? The day is slipping away. As I was saying, we are right near Magic Kingdom so why not just head over there? We're going to want to see everything, right? We might as well start there, n'est-ce pas?"

Max gave her a smirk. "Nest pah?" he asked.

"No," she said. "N'est-ce pas. It's French. It means, 'isn't that true'?"

He stared at her for a moment and then laughed out loud. "Okay," he said. "I think I'm going to take German next year. That'll show you."

"Right," she said. "Back to the question." She pulled a Map of the Magic Kingdom out of her knapsack, which doubled as a purse.

"What question?" he asked.

"The one you asked," she said. "You asked, 'what do we want to do?'"

"Oh, yeah," said Max. "Well? Actually, Kenz, I think it was you who asked that question."

"OK, maybe. Anyway, how about we start on 'Space Mountain', then 'the Seven Dwarves Mine Ride', and do

'Tomorrow Land', okay?"

Max couldn't keep from laughing out loud at his sister's obvious excitement. "Sure," he said. "Let's eat and then go."

"What's so funny?" she asked.

"Nothing, nothing at all," Max assured her with a smirk on his face.

Before she could ask another question, Max phoned Gina and Colby, who told them they were on their way and would join them shortly. McKenzie shut down her own phone, placed in her pocket, and fingered the medallion around her neck.

McKenzie started to ask, "So why did you insist we bring these to...". Her question was interrupted.

And their lives were suddenly changed forever.

CHAPTER 8

A tall man walked over to their table. He smiled at them, and the twins felt a warm comfortable peace envelope them.

"Hello, Beloved," said the Man. "May I join you?"

"Er…" began Max, "Curiel, is that you?"

"Uh…" stammered McKenzie. "Do you know this man, Max?"

"Well, sort of…w-w-we kind of met in front of the school one d-d-d-day," Max stuttered; something he had not done for awhile.

"Why are you so nervous?" persisted Kenzie. "What's going on?"

"I'm sure Max has told you about our visit," asserted Curiel, his eyes boring into Max's.

"Uhh, well, I was going to," mumbled Max. "I mean I haven't had the chance...I thought once we got in the parks...I did remember to have her bring her amulet and I have mine," he responded, fumbling for an excuse.

"It is no matter. She will understand soon enough. Please take out your amulets and hold them up, Beloved," said the Man. McKenzie and Max exchanged glances, then obeyed by removing them from around their necks. As they held them up, an expanding circle of light appeared. They reached out, took the man's hands in their own, and passed through the circle of light.

CHAPTER 9

The twins felt a strange sensation of moving through the air, of flashing lights, and weird harmonies of music, all unlike those they had ever experienced. When the sensation stopped, they found themselves in front of a large stone building, with minimal lights and overpowering darkness.

"Take a few moments, Beloved," said the Tall Man. "Take a few deep breaths and let yourselves adjust."

The twins looked at one another, and took deep breaths. Their heads stopped spinning at once, and their eyes cleared and focused.

"What is happening? Where are we, Sir?" asked McKenzie.

"Remember how you thought we were in for a big adventure on this vacation, Kenz? Well, I think this may be the beginning of one," whispered Max.

"You have come with me to Ancient Israel," said the Man.

The twins looked at one another, then at the man, then at the huge building. The Man noticed how their gestures were so similar, so much alike. "You are like many other sets of twins I have met," remarked the Man. "You have almost a sixth sense of what the other is thinking and doing."

"That's true," said Max and Gina together.

"Yes. Other people have mentioned how similar we are in actions. But we make a point of not wearing the same colors, or the same clothing styles. But it would have been nice to have been told about the existence of this Man and your meeting with him," she said, oozing frustration and staring pointedly at her brother.

"I don't really know all that much, Kenzie," said Max, in his own defense.

"Exactly, who are you, Sir?" questioned Kenzie.

"I am a friend of your sister and her husband, as well as their friends Marina and Dan. My name is Curiel, as you, Max, are aware."

All of a sudden things made sense to the twins. "Curiel!" said McKenzie, and suddenly things clicked as she recalled some stories her sister had told them years ago.

"He's an Angel, aren't you?" said Max, directing his gaze at his sister.

"Yes," said the Man, smiling. "I am an Archangel. You didn't recognize me in a different context. McKenzie, we haven't met, I know, but Colby and Gina know me well."

"You took them on many adventures, haven't you," noted Max. Then it struck him. "That's what we're doing here in ancient Israel, isn't it?"

"Exactly right," explained Curiel. "I am here to offer you the opportunity for a once-in-a-lifetime adventure."

"Offer?" questioned McKenzie.

"You mean, we don't have to do this thing?" asked Max. "Whatever it is."

"That is correct," said Curiel. "I am merely here to offer you the opportunity."

"Can one of us accept and the other reject the offer?" asked Max.

"Max!" snapped McKenzie. "Will you stop being difficult?"

"I don't mean that's what I'm going to do, Kenz," muttered

Max.

"Then why ask?" challenged his sister, and the two of them assumed aggressive postures, ready to have one of their typical quarrels with one another.

"No," corrected Curiel. "You mustn't quarrel. You two do that often, and all it does is upset you, make your stomachs hurt, and occasionally be moved to tears."

" I guess that's true, sir," agreed McKenzie.

The twins looked at Him, then at one another, and then the ground. "That's true. But we have improved in that area, for the most part, sir," said Max defensively.

"Can you explain it?" said the Angel.

Max shrugged, which was his standard reply to any question when he didn't want to face the obvious truth in a situation.

"Yes, it is obvious," said the Angel. Max's head jerked up. He realized that Curiel knew what he was thinking.

"Okay," said Max. "I guess—"

"You know," corrected Curiel.

"Yeah," he admitted. "Sometimes I get jealous of McKenzie."

"We've always competed with one another, not always cooperated," confessed McKenzie. Her cheeks were red with embarrassment.

"That is true, Beloved," said the Angel.

"I think we have always competed for attention, for affection, and been jealous of gifts that the other has received," agreed Max. He felt that he was expressing himself better, thinking more clearly, feeling more alert.

"Now we are moving toward the truth, Beloved," encouraged the Angel. "Do you see that you could do much better if you cooperated, grieved for one another's failures, and rejoiced in one another's successes?"

Now their embarrassment increased. The twins nodded in unison, as if the action was choreographed. Their heads were downcast and they didn't see the angel smiling. "Well," said Curiel, pleased. "I believe you have come under the influence of this place."

"What is this place?" asked McKenzie.

"Beloved, this is Solomon's temple," instructed Curiel. "You are having difficulty being dishonest with one another because the native language of this Temple is truth. We are in the distant past, just before an invading army will come to destroy this place." Their was a tone of sadness in his voice.

"This beautiful Temple is about to be destroyed?" asked Max, aghast.

"Yes, Beloved," nodded Curiel. "Some of your historians considered this place to be one of the Seven Wonders of the Ancient World. The precision of the masonry, the magnificence of the structure, the beauty of the interior, and the exquisite furnishings will never be duplicated. Other, and lesser, temples will be built here, but none will equal the magnificence of this one."

"So, when you asked us about how we quarrel," said Max, "we didn't have a choice in telling ourselves the truth?"

"Oh yes, of course you did," said Curiel. "You are young enough that your instinct for truth is still strong within you. In your later years, you will be motivated to tell the truth by a desire to serve the One whose name you bear. You will not need to stand in this temple."

"Excuse me, Mr. Curiel," asked Max. "Why are we here?"

"Your friend Marina and her husband transported here using the Amulets that now are in your possession. I met them in the Inner Room, which is called 'the Holy of Holies'. They helped the prophet Jeremiah remove the great treasures of the Holy of Holies, and aided in hiding them as well," said Curiel. "We want you to see where the treasures were hidden as the armies advanced. Then, when the time is right, you will come back here and help recover them for the Israeli temple."

"What do you mean by the Holy of Holies?" asked Max.

"That was the place behind that curtain that was reserved for the presence of God, and therefore, the most holy place in the temple," explained Curiel.

"Did the people of Israel ever get to see the great treasures?" said McKenzie.

"Very few," said Curiel. "In all the history of Israel, other than right at the beginning during their creation, the only one who ever saw these treasures was the High Priest, who was always a descendant of Levi, Jacob's sons and grandsons; that is, until tonight. And, of course, you are privileged to see these unique antiquities of history."

McKenzie's eyes were wide with amazement. "I don't know what to say. I mean, all this is just so, so gorgeous. And you are telling us this beautiful temple will be destroyed?"

"What will happen on this night?" asked Max.

"Tonight they are moving the treasures to a safe location. An Egyptian Pharaoh named Shishak has begun to send his troops against the Temple and the people of Israel," explained Curiel. "It won't happen tonight, as we stand here. However, the Egyptians will come against this place in a few days, or perhaps weeks, and the Israelis will not be able to withstand their onslaught."

"I remember the movie *Raiders of the Lost Ark*," said Max. "It's one of my favorite films.

"It was a terrific film," said McKenzie. "I loved it too. We've probably seen it five or six times."

"The film didn't have a correct depiction of the Ark and where it was hidden though," said Curiel. "Shishak and the Egyptians did not steal or profane them. The treasures were hidden near here, though outside the great wall. Now just watch."

The twins, accompanied by their angel friend, now stood at the foot of a flight of steps which led up to an enormous curtain, about 60 feet high, forty feet wide, and about a foot thick. Obviously, it was covering a room, and the twins could not see inside. "Curiel, is the Holy of Holies behind that curtain?" asked McKenzie.

"Yes, indeed," said the Angel. "Your friend Marina and her friend Dan are helping Jeremiah."

"Jeremiah?" asked McKenzie. "The prophet from the Bible."

"Yes, beloved," said Curiel. "They are helping him wrap the great treasures. They are coming. Hide beneath my cloak. They mustn't see you now."

The twins placed themselves beneath the cloak, which apparently had no weight. They realized that they could see out, but people could not see them, nor could they see the Angel who wore it.

"Oh my gosh," exclaimed Max. "Look, it's Marina, and there's Dan! How is this possible?"

Someone had pulled the huge Veil across the entrance to the Holy of Holies aside and Marina and Dan came out. They helped the priests who were struggling to remove the great treasures that had not budged from the room for many years. McKenzie saw that Marina and Dan were assigned to carry a huge candlestick.

"Curiel," whispered Max. The angel turned, anticipating his question. "That candlestick looks like it is really heavy. I mean Marina and Dan look like they are having a lot of trouble carrying it."

"It is permissible to speak, Max. The cloak also prevents our voices from being heard by others. The candlestick is made of solid gold," reminded the Angel. "So, yes, the two of them are having some difficulty attempting to remove it."

"*Solid* gold?" mumbled Max. "No wonder it's so heavy."

"Yes, Max," continued Curiel. "When the children of Israel came out of Egypt, the people who had imprisoned them were prompted by the God of Israel to give them all their gold as the Jews were leaving their captivity. They came to the Promised Land carrying that gold. You'll recall that at one point, they used some of the gold to create a golden calf."

"I remember the story," nodded McKenzie. "I think some people believe that Moses had the people grind the idol to gold dust and then forced the people to drink it."

"Exactly," said Curiel. "And then, later, the expert craftsman named Bezalel used the rest of the gold to construct the great treasures in the Holy of Holies."

"What are all those things in there besides the Ark and the candlesticks?"

"Two large statues of Cherubim," began the Angel.

"Statues of what?" asked Max.

"Cherubim are heavenly creatures," said Curiel. "They are

difficult to describe. The word is plural. Cherub refers to one of the creatures; cherubim are two or more."

"Oh, I see," said Max.

Curiel continued, "The wings of the cherubim statues covered the ark. Also, there is a golden altar of incense and many other other golden and silver objects. In fact, the book of Ezra in the bible tells us there were 5400 objects made of gold and silver in the temple in Jerusalem."

"Whoa! The articles in that room must be incredibly valuable then, right?" McKenzie exclaimed.

"In many ways, McKenzie, yes. But the value to them was more symbolic than monetary. In other words, what it represented to them spiritually, I mean, as a way to honor God, was what was valuable about the objects."

Max had been silent for a few moments, focusing on what he was seeing. "Curiel," he asked, "are we being assigned to recover those treasures if they still exist?"

"I suspect the Almighty might be asking for your help with recovering the objects, yes," said Curiel.

"Will you be allowed to help us?" asked Max.

"I will do what I can," said Curiel. "Understand, these objects are man-made and hidden by man, so I cannot intervene as we might like."

"Phooey," groaned Max.

"That's too bad," said McKenzie.

"But let us not worry about that now," said Curiel. "It is time for you to return to your hotel. Be alert and ready, but for now, enjoy yourselves. We have no time limit, beloved."

"Yes sir," said Max.-And they again found themselves at a table in the Kona Cafe, staring at McKenzie's pancake order and

Max's Tonga Toast. "What on earth?" gasped Max, out of breath.

"I don't know," said his twin sister, "That was what... ....weird, scary, exciting, unbelievable?"

Max glanced at his watch, a Christmas present from last year, which he considered his prized possession. Now, it had gone to ancient Jerusalem, and hadn't lost a second. "We seem to have stepped out of time," he reported, astonishment ringing in his voice. "According to my watch, no time at all went by."

McKenzie stared at him. "But I know we were gone for more than an hour at least," she insisted. "We walked all around the old temple, watched some of the treasures being carried out of the Holy of Holies."

"What about the Holy of Holies?" asked a voice at McKenzie's elbow.

The twins looked up and saw that their sister Gina and her husband Colby had walked up.

"Gina," said Max. "Did we disappear for a few seconds?"

Gina and Colby laughed. "You mean, like hocus-pocus?" asked their sister.

"No," asserted McKenzie. "But I am sure we have been gone for at least an hour, maybe more."

"Gone?" said Colby. "Gone where?" The adults looked concerned now.

"We went to ancient Jerusalem," explained Max, excitement evident in his voice. "We went with Curiel."

"Oh, of course, the Archangel," Gina exclaimed.

"That's great," encouraged Colby. "He is an old and dear friend. Remember, if he's involved in your adventure, you certainly have nothing to fear. Nothing whatever."

Gina and Colby sat down at the table with the twins as a

waitress came over with the French press coffee that Colby had ordered. They turned to the twins. "Tell us," said Gina.

The twins' minds seem to be whirling as they struggled to relate what had happened when they stepped out of their own time. "And we saw Marina and Dan, also," said Max. "It was totally weird."

"Really? What were they doing?" asked Colby.

"We saw them carrying a solid gold candlestick down the steps outside the Holy of Holies," said McKenzie. "It was really heavy."

"Where were you?" asked Gina.

"We were standing next to a huge altar," said Max. "Curiel told us to stand under his cloak and watch from there."

"Right," said Gina, and she seemed puzzled.

"I get it," announced Colby. The others turned to him. Gina raised an eyebrow. "Yeah," he continued. "If they'd seen you, they'd probably wouldn't have recognized you. Think about it."

"Good point," said Gina. "Yeah. When they had that adventure, you two were barely seven years old. You've changed a lot in the last several years. At that time they only knew you as six-or seven-years old."

"Okay," said Max. "Anyhow, I doubt the archangel wanted to cause any confusion at that time for the people."

"Yes, Marina has vivid memories of that night," said Gina. "They worked their brains out. They were exhausted when they finished helping to carry the stuff out in order to hide it from the invaders."

"Do they remember where they took it?" asked Max.

Gina and Colby looked at one another. They opened their mouths to speak, but then shut them again. "No, they don't," said Gina. "They did tell us that at one point they crawled through one of the small gates of Jerusalem."

"One gate, right," said Colby. "It had a name, too. Something about a needle."

"He's right," said Gina. "I remember now. The wall of Jerusalem had a small door called the 'Eye of the Needle.' It was there so that the city could be closed off almost completely. This door would allow only one person through at a time, and not an army or horses. By the way, both Marina and Dan said that the Ark was one of the most beautiful works of art they've ever seen."

"It must have been huge, I think," said Colby.

"We only got a glimpse inside but what I think may have been the Ark was quite beautiful but it was pretty dark, so we didn't get to see much, at least not clearly. So, I suppose the movie wasn't accurate, huh?" remarked Max. "I mean, *Raiders of the Lost Ark*."

"No, probably not," laughed Colby. "It weighed a lot. I think it took eight Levite priests to move it.

"It was a thrill to see what we were able. The temple was so magnificent," sighed McKenzie.

"It would have been a thrill to see all the temple treasures," agreed Gina.

"Do you think they're hidden still?" asked Max. "I mean, some people think that they were stolen and melted down, you know?"

"I guess they *could* have been destroyed," said Colby. "The chances that they've survived all this time are not guaranteed. Still, I think the Israelis would have found a way to protect them if there was any way possible to do that. These were the greatest treasures of their nation."

"You know, now that you mention it, that could be why they haven't been found," said Gina. "The Hebrews, I think, may have trusted that God would reveal them once again when the time was right. So he kept their location secret even from the people of Israel."

At this point, Colby and Gina greeted the wait staff of the Kona Cafe who brought them their lunches. When they were settled, McKenzie continued the conversation, "Why can't they remember where the temple treasures are?"

"I don't know for sure," said Colby. "But think about it. This was long ago and if they had hidden them from invading armies they would have told as few people as possible to keep them safe. Then years go by, many people probably died carrying the secret with them, and finally all that information is lost. My guess is that Gina is right; they're not supposed to remember it or a discovery would have been made."

"Let's eat," Gina said. "We can continue this later. It is a lot to think about."

The group ate their lunch and chatted about their room at the Polynesian, their plans for the afternoon, and where to meet up later. At last Gina consulted her watch. "I made dinner reservations at the Grand Floridian Hotel," she said. "We have to be there by 7:00 P.M. That'll give you two about six hours in the Magic Kingdom, okay?"

"We're on our way and we'll see you later!" Max announced as he and Kenzie stood to catch the monorail.

"All right," said Gina. "Look, don't worry about this business with the ark and the other treasures. I do know that you'll never be asked to do more than you can handle."

"What we're asking *now* is that you be on time for dinner," interrupted Colby, grinning.

"Yes, yes," yelled Kenzie, waving as the twins were running out the door. "The Grand Floridian Cafe. We will be there."

CHAPTER 10

The day was perfect, considering it was 18* back home, and the twins entered the Magic Kingdom with enthusiasm. It took a conscious effort not to stop along Main Street to check out everything. "Hey, Kenz," said Max, "maybe we should stop over there and get something at the Main Street Bakery, you know, in case we get hungry later." He was never one to miss a chance for a sweet snack.

McKenzie moaned. "We just finished eating moments ago. NO, we are not stopping!" She hustled him along, and soon they arrived at their first agreed upon destination: *Space Mountain*. The line was minimal, and soon they were zooming up and down in the dark, McKenzie screaming with pleasure and Max trying not to be terrified. After that ride, they stood in line for a half hour in order to ride another roller coaster, *The Seven Dwarves Mine Train,* which was a much gentler ride than *Space Mountain*. The lines were much longer for this ride because it was relatively new but they didn't mind because of the three interactive games to play as the line moved along. The theming was quite clever and they got the feeling of being in the mine of the seven dwarves. Max even got to see Snow White appear playing the third game with the barrels.

After the mine train they hurried toward the Adventure Land section of the park.

As they approached *Peter Pan's Flight*, McKenzie shouted, "Oh, Max, let's go on this."

"You want to wait in line to go on Peter Pan? A ride for little kids? Come on, let's find something else."

"Pleasssssse," she begged. "I think it has been redone since we were here last and I have always loved the book, 'Peter Pan'. It won't take long."

"Right", grumbled Max, "it looks like this line is even longer than the one for the Seven Dwarves Mine Train." But he grudgingly agreed. "Okay, but you owe me one." She bobbed her head up and down to let him know she understood and they entered the line which consisted mostly of very young children. *At least it's not one of those stomach churning roller coasters*, Max thought to himself.

After Peter Pan they continued on to the Adventure Land, and soon clambered onto a roller coaster called *Big Thunder Railroad*, which became a favorite for both of them. Even Max, not as fond of roller coasters as his sister, enjoyed the highly detailed set, the unusual props, and even extended his arms up in the air while riding in the little mine train car.

On the other hand, he could not help but notice that McKenzie had a terrific time on all the Magic Kingdom roller coasters. Again Max was struck by how different he was from his sister in this respect. They had been born within ten minutes of one another, but their parents would never tell them who was born first. There were always plenty of things for them to argue about without giving one of them the ability to declare "Well, I *am* the oldest." A while ago they had once again tried to get this information out of their parents.

"All we have to do is check our birth certificates," suggested Max.

"Yeah, that's right," said McKenzie.

"So you know where we keep them?" asked Dad, with a twinkle in his eyes.

"Er…" said Max glancing over to McKenzie.

"Well, no…" said his sister.

"Someday," promised their mother. "Meantime, just think about being born at the same time, okay?"

"But why?" whined McKenzie.

"No," said Dad. "No, no, no. You two are so competitive with one another that you'll never stop arguing even if we tell you. No," he went on. "Someday, we'll tell you."

The twins grumped at the time, but it did little good. The exact timing of their birth remained a family mystery.

The twins had little trouble getting on the rest of the rides that afternoon since the crowds were a little lighter this time of year. Colby glanced at his watch and announced, "Hey, we need to leave if we are going to be on time to meet Gina and Colby."

As they scooted their way around the people, they came to *The Pirates of the Caribbean* and again, Kenzie insisted they ride before leaving. "Come on, Max, there's not even a line. We can whisk in and out in no time." Max was not so sure about the accuracy of her statement since long lines could still be out of sight through the doorway beyond. So they moved forward and were rewarded with no waiting time and a fun ride reminding them of several scenes from the film of the same name. Captain Jack played a prominent role in the sets as they floated through the canal.

They finally made their way to the park exit and onto the monorail, bound for the Grand Floridian Resort.

Their sister and her husband sat just outside the restaurant in the lounge area awaiting their arrival. Colby walked up to the hostess and tell her that their party had all arrived and soon they were seated, menus in hand, trying to decide on dinner choices.

In the end, both Max and McKenzie ordered the 'Surf and Turf Burger' after the server promised they would love it, and Colby and Gina both ordered the 'Shrimp and Grits'. No one was disappointed. Twice Kenzie asked for more of the red onion marmalade for her burger and Colby kept making yummy noises over his cheesy grits despite his wife giving him a poke in the ribs. They ordered two of the Chocolate Fondue desserts to split between the four of the them and devoured every morsel. "Wow, I guess I was more hungry than I thought," announced Max, licking chocolate off his fingers. His sisters looked at one another and rolled their eyes. Max's appetite had been a legend in the family for quite a while.

"Hey, I have a great idea," announced Gina. "Today at my conference I was talking to this lady who has an annual pass here and she suggested we walk out to the restaurant over there, Narcossee's, and watch the Magic Kingdom fireworks from the outside deck. She promised we wouldn't be disappointed in the view." They all jumped on that idea and strolled out to the viewing area suggested by the woman. After all the ooohing and aahhhing over the fireworks, they trudged back to the monorail and exited at the Polynesian Resort.

They had adjoining rooms so Gina and Colby unlocked their door and they all entered with Max and McKenzie continuing into their room. "Don't stay up too late," warned Gina. "You want to be able to get up at a decent hour."

"I don't think you need to worry about that," said Kenzie, yawning. The twins showered and changed, thrilled that they each had their own double bed. They each checked their messages for the day and replied to the ones they felt important, turned on the T.V., and flipped channels for a few minutes. "Can we just turn this off," pleaded Gina, "I am really tired all of a sudden." So Max silenced the T.V., they both plugged in their devices, turned out the lights, and lay there for a few moments talking about the plans for the next day. Within minutes, both fell into a deep sleep.

CHAPTER 11

They both woke suddenly. The room was dark and quiet, and an eerie glow from a nightlight glowed in the washroom. "Kenz?" whispered Max. "Are you awake?"

"Yes," she said. "What woke us up?"

Max pressed the light button on his watch. "3:00 A. M.," he grumbled. "Are you sleepy?"

"No," McKenzie replied. "Not a bit. I'm thinking we both awoke at the same time for a reason, though."

"Quite right, Beloved," said a voice they recognized. A dull light at the foot of their beds began to grow in intensity and expand in size.

"Curiel!" they said in unison.

"Yes, Beloved," he said. "I see your medallions are around your neck. Good. That will save time having to search for them. Come with me." He stretched out his hands and the twins found themselves on a plain, watching some sort of procession.

"What are we watching?" asked McKenzie.

"It is important for your to understand the consequences if the Ark falls into the wrong hands. What you are viewing here has taken place a few hundred years before our last visit. You are witnessing a time when the Philistine army is returning to their homeland in triumph after defeating Israel in a brutal battle," explained Curiel. "They have stolen the Ark and are carrying it back to their city."

"Can they do that?" asked McKenzie, aghast.

"Well, they believe they can," said Curiel, "But they will not like how this turns out for them. Pay close attention." The air swirled around them and they found themselves in some sort of a huge temple. A gigantic, grotesque idol stood at one end of the temple. The statue revolted the twins just to look at it.

"What is that ugly thing?" asked Max.

"The name of the god is Dagon, and at this time he was the Chief God of the Philistines. Dagon had the head and upper body of a man. His lower parts are those of a fish."

"You mean they actually worshipped that whatever it is? " asked Max.

"I know, it seems hard for you to believe," said Curiel, "but Dagon was their god of fertility and crops. Worship of this god played a big role in way that the Philistines looked at ideas of death and the afterlife."

"He, I mean, the statue is hideous," said McKenzie.

"Yech," agreed Max.

"The Philistines worshipped Dagon and asked him for victory in war by offering different sorts of sacrifices for his favor. Here, you see that they have presented him with the Ark as a thank you gift for what they believe was his assistance in winning the battle."

"But isn't that kind of ridiculous," said McKenzie. "How could these people ever think something like this could be a god? Seems kind of stupid."

"No, you are quite right," agreed Curiel. "He is a statue, not an spiritual being. But your observation comes from the advantage of living in the era in which you were born and the knowledge you have gained. Their worship was in vain, but to them it was perfectly logical. In the Philistine pantheon, that is, the list of their gods, Dagon was at the top of the list. Both the Philistines and the broader Canaanite society held him in reverence and considered him a crucial force in their lives. Still, you are correct. Dagon is certainly not worthy of worship."

"Why did they put the Ark in here, in the dark, in front of him?"

"Because they are choosing to believe that Dagon is real, and that he gave them victory over the Israelis, and therefore they present what they consider to be an incredibly valuable trophy in front of him."

"My gosh," murmured Max.

"Now, come ahead to the next morning with me," said the Angel.

The air swirled around them and in the next minute they stood outside the Temple of Dagon. It was just after dawn and they saw temple priests marching toward the temple. "What are they singing?" asked McKenzie.

"Songs of praise to Dagon," returned the Angel.

"That is just so weird," said McKenzie. "I still can't imagine why they would they choose to worship a monster."

"They live in fear," explained Curiel, and he displayed not the slightest impatience with the twins' questions. "They are terrified of the priests, of the god, Dagon, itself, of possible retribution by the gods, of many other things. This is why they offer these sacrifices."

"You mean they do it to keep the demon gods happy, not out of a sense of devotion or gratitude," reasoned Max. Curiel nodded in agreement.

As the twins watched, the priestly procession had almost finished entering the temple when a dreadful scream went up.

Then several Priests, their robes flying and their eyes wild, came running from the temple.

"What is it?" demanded a man wearing beautiful robes, obviously a person of great power.

"My liege," yelled the Chief Priest. "Come and see! It's terrible!"

The King hitched up his robes and ran into the temple.

"Do you wish to see, Beloved?" asked Curiel.

Together, the twins responded, "Yes," and in the next second, they stood inside the temple, well off the side so that they could see what was going on. No one could mistake the panic on the faces of the priests.

"Look at Dagon!" cried Max, pointing at the idol.

"It's fallen over on its face," said McKenzie. "It's lying in front of the Ark and his hands are broken off at the wrists."

"Yes, Beloved," smiled Curiel. "Now let us move forward a few months."

This time they appeared into a large room. Five men in splendid garments stood in front arguing with one another. The twins, safe underneath Curiel's cloak, saw that the men had what looked like welts or swelling all over their body. "Curiel!" she gasped. "What's wrong with them?"

"Because they have taken the Ark, the Lord has caused the whole town to be struck with tumors all over their bodies, but they do not have a name for this and are scared," said the Angel. "Removing the Ark has caused some problems for them, as you see."

"What are they talking about?" asked Max. "Are they trying to figure out what the rash on their faces is?"

Curiel gave them a slight smile. "The Ark has been sent from city to city and in each place, dreadful things have happened. Plagues, skin sores, famines, tumors and death were just a few of them. So they've now decided to send the Ark back to Israel."

"What is that?" asked Max, pointing to what looked like a small wagon drawn by two milk cows.

"It's a cart, like a farm wagon," said Curiel. "It is brand new, and has never been used. The animals are milk cows, which don't haul oxcarts. Look! Here comes the Ark." Several large men carried the Ark with ten foot poles thrust through the carry rings. The men came forward and lifted the Ark onto the cart. The Angel continued to stand with his cloak wrapped around the two teenagers.

A man who, by his clothing, his bearing and the way the other Philistines spoke and deferred to him, must be the High King of their nation, came forward. Keeping a respectful distance from the Ark, he spoke in a ringing voice. "We wish to test the events of the last few months. If the cattle walk with the Ark up to Israel, we can know the God of the Israelis did this. However, if the cattle do not walk the Ark up to Israel, we will know that these events happened just by chance."

"By chance? Right!" exclaimed the twins in unison, rolling their eyes at that suggestion. But the rest of the Philistine kings and their people were nodding their heads in agreement with the High King.

"So they think that this disease and disaster that has come upon them could be nothing more than a gambling result?" asked Max.

"Yes," said Curiel. "They are, you see, people who don't truly believe in any god, including the True God of the Hebrews, or any of the monsters of their belief system. What they really believe in is luck, or chance, which is of course nothing at all. Nothing. They are, as you see, people without any real god."

"I don't understand," said Max.

Curiel grasped their hands and explained. "If you hold a long straw and a short straw, McKenzie, and you ask Max to pull one out of your hands, what are the possibilities that he will draw the short straw or the long straw?"

The twins exchanged glances. "Is it 50 percent?"

"No," smiled the Angel. "Think again. It is almost a trick question."

Max suddenly got the joke. "Okay, right. The odds that you will pull out the long straw _or_ the short straw are 100%, unless you don't participate. You have to get one or the other."

"Correct," said the Angel. "Try again. If you flip a coin, what are the odds that the coin will come up either heads or tails?"

"Okay," said McKenzie. "I get it. It has to land on _either_ heads or tails."

"Right," said the Angel. "Do you see what I mean?"

"So there is no such thing as Chance," said Max.

"Right," smiled Curiel. "People like to use the word 'luck', as well, as if _it_ had some magic powers to change or alter a situation. But it doesn't, because 'luck' doesn't exist. In this situation here, the cows would either walk up to Israel or they wouldn't. However these cows had a specific purpose to their lives, do you see?"

"I bet they walk right up to Israel," declared Max. The Angel and McKenzie grinned at him.

By this time, they had followed the cows almost into Israel, and they saw some Israeli farmers working in their fields. When the Israelis saw what was in the cart the cattle were pulling, they dispatched a man to summon the authorities of their village and the army.

"The cattle won't stop until they reach Jerusalem, I bet," said McKenzie. Now her brother and the angel chuckled.

In a few moments, though, the priests and the army, as well as many of the people in the area came, singing and rejoicing, to retrieve the Ark. "Come, beloved," said Curiel. "I do not wish for you to see the rest. The Israelis will sacrifice the cows as a thank offering to God. You are not accustomed to the blood of a sacrifice and it would be difficult for you to watch."

"You mean they'll kill the cows?" asked Max, and both the twins found themselves feeling bad for the animals. "But they didn't do anything! If it wasn't for the cows the Ark would not have even made it back to Israel!"

"Yes," said Curiel. "Remember that in these days, sacrifice of animals was an expression of joy and pleasure and worship to God, not a malicious and evil act. Animal sacrifice was part of the Hebrew worship service. In this case, the Almighty directed the cows to bring the Ark back where it belongs. Now, they will serve another purpose, a willing sacrifice intended to praise God."

Lights and beautiful sounds again swirled around them and they were aware of a lovely smell, as in a greenhouse of roses and other fragrant flowers.

"What have you learned?" questioned Curiel.

The twins found themselves standing in a beautiful field, with large trees nearby. The breeze was warm and gentle, and a stream ran a few feet away. "I'm so thirsty. May we drink from the stream?" Max asked.

"Yes, please do," encouraged the Angel. When the twins

drank the water, any lingering sadness and dismay vanished from their hearts, and the gentle warmth they felt when they were near their Angel friend returned.

"What, now, have you learned?" Curiel again asked.

McKenzie spoke up. "I saw how much the Ark meant to the people of Israel. I didn't understand, I guess."

"Well," added Max, "I think it showed us what a terrible thing it would be if even today the wrong people end up finding the Ark. Lots of people could die. I'm guessing it should only be recovered by the Jewish people."

"Very good," agreed the Angel. "The temple, or temples, in Jerusalem meant a great deal to the people. Still they did not worship the Ark. It was a symbol of the relationship of Israel to the creator. Also a reminder of all He had done for them and where their God was to reside in the temple during that era of their civilization. This relationship is called a *Covenant.*"

"Is there something more that we understand about the Ark?" asked Max.

Curiel sat on the grass looking at the stream. The twins came and sat next to him, staring at a distant range of mountains.

"Is that what the words in the song *America The Beautiful* mean when they refer to 'purple mountains majesty?'" asked McKenzie. "I mean, these mountains kind of look purple in this light."

"Yes," said the Angel. "They are beautiful, aren't they?"

"I feel, I don't know, *warm* when I look at them," agreed Max.

"Yes," said the Angel. "You are with me, sitting on the side of life which loves that which pure, that which is right, that which is joyful. Always look for the beauty in life."

The twins nodded. "You need to understand the meaning of a symbol," remarked their friend.

"I think it has to do with how things, I mean, objects, can have meaning to us as humans," said Max. "We give certain things meaning, and they help us understand ideas."

"Very good," said the Angel. "You are going to be studying symbols in life and literature as you continue your education. And once more, consider the Ark of the Covenant."

"Tell us about what a covenant is," urged Max. The Angel nodded.

"Do you remember what your sister Gina said when she got married?" asked Curiel. "You two stood with her as she married Colby."

"Were you there also, Curiel?" asked McKenzie.

"I certainly was," he smiled. "I was very proud of both of them. Anyhow, do you remember that their marriage consisted of promises to one another and to God?"

"Yes," said Max. "I don't remember the exact words, but they promised to love one another until—" Max grew silent. Curiel put his arm around the boy, who suddenly felt like he might cry. He glanced at his sister, and saw that her eyes had also moistened.

"It is all right," said Curiel. "Both of you love your sister and want her to be happy for the rest of her life. I'm pretty sure she will be. I cannot see the future, but I can feel her heart, and I know how much she loves Colby."

"Right," said McKenzie, who wiped at her cheeks. She did indeed love her sister and looked up to her as a role model.

"Consider those vows for a second," said Curiel. "Do you remember how long those vows will be in effect?"

"I want to say forever," said Max. "But I don't think that's right. I think they promised to stay married until they are separated by death.

"That's correct," said the Angel. "They took what are called *vows*. A covenant is different. It lasts forever."

"How can a promise last forever?" said McKenzie. "People die, and…wait. God doesn't die."

"That's right," said Curiel. "So covenants extends beyond death. Covenants apply to the children, grandchildren and great grandchildren, on and on, forever."

"But with Gina," said McKenzie, struggling to understand, "she and Colby took vows, which only apply as long as they are both alive."

"Precisely right," grinned Curiel. "When one of them dies, the other is free from the vow. But...," he turned and motioned to Max.

Max understood. "When God makes a covenant with a nation, it is supposed to continue through all the generations that come along," said Max, his eyes lighting.

"So, what does that have to do with the Ark of the Covenant?" asked Curiel.

"I get it," said Max. "The Ark was, is, a reminder, a symbol, to the people of Israel that they are still bound to God by a promise that goes from generation to generation."

"Very good," said the Angel. "Do you remember what is inside the Ark?"

"Yes," said McKenzie. "I think it contains the tablets of the promise, or Covenant, God made with Israel through Moses."

Curiel smiled. "Until later, Beloved." And then he vanished.

Then lights flashed and cleared, and the twins found

themselves in their beds at the Polynesian Resort. "Are you two okay?" asked their sister Gina, who had come to stand in the doorway between their two rooms.

"Yes, Gina," said McKenzie. "We were just…er…talking."

"At three in the morning?" said Gina.

"Well, " said Max. "Well, not exactly."

Their sister came over and sat down on McKenzie's bed. "What happened?"

Now her husband came into the room. "What's up, you two? When we told you to be up early we didn't mean quite this early," he said, laughing.

The twins looked back and forth, and then Max nodded to McKenzie. "Okay," she said. "We'll tell you."

For the next ten minutes the twins talked to their sister and brother-in-law about what they had seen and what had happened. The couple encouraged Max and Kenzie to relate the details of their visit by asking occasional questions.

"Well," said Colby, "it sure seems you have a decision to make, don't you."

The twins exchanged glances. "What do you mean?"

"If you continue with this adventure, you could be in some danger," explained Gina.

"Yes, we could," they agreed.

"But, life is about making such decisions," said Gina. "Everything worthwhile implies taking some sort of risk."

"I guess that's true," considered Max.

"Well, when I went to apply to veterinary college after I got my bachelor's degree, I had to decide if I wanted to take the chance of being rejected," Gina shrugged. "I earned good grades in college, but it was still a risk."

Her husband snorted. "It wasn't that much of a risk," he smiled, and he had an expression of pride on his face. "Your sister was number two in her class at vet school. Her professors told me they thought she was brilliant."

"Colby," said Gina, indignant at his remark. "I certainly felt it was risky at the time. Besides, it was a huge investment of time and money and I had no guarantees how it would turn out!" Looking directly at the twins she said, "We, Colby and I, had to make the same kind of decision. Actually, I believe anyone who is offered one of these adventures must decide if they are willing to take the risk of injury in order to gain something greater."

"Another example," he said. "I think about the risk Marina took at the Red Sea. That is a great illustration."

"What are you talking about?" questioned Max.

"Marina took a risk at the Red Sea?" said McKenzie.

"You never told us about that," said Max.

"Well, it's a long story, and some day she will have to tell you all the details," smiled Colby, "but Marina and Dan participated in an adventure where they helped the Israelites in crossing the Red Sea. The land masses were connected by a natural bridge that went about two hundred feet below the surface. On either side of the land bridge the sea floor dropped off to several thousand feet."

"That deep?" said McKenzie.

"At one point," said Gina, picking up the story, "she witnessed a small child slip off the land bridge where they were crossing and disappear into the depths of the Red Sea. You see, on each side of the land bridge were tall walls of water that seemed to be held upright by an invisible shield and the child could see all these fascinating sea creatures swimming. When he reached out to grab one...."

"He fell through the wall of water?" reasoned McKenzie, horrified, as she finished the sentence Colby had started.

"That's right," continued Gina, "without a thought for her own safety she dove in and rescued the child.

"With the aid of a friendly dolphin," added Colby. Gina smiled in agreement.

"Well, the truly amazing thing was that little boy was named Zadok, and his family was from the clan of the Levites, the tribe appointed to be the priests for the nation. It seems that the child they saved was probably one of the ancestors of the high priest of King David of the bible."

"So if Marina hadn't been there, I mean if she had refused her adventure, Zadok would have died and David's reign could have been different!" exclaimed McKenzie.

"Yes, it seems at least possible," said Colby. "You just never know what impact your actions might have on future events, how your life might affect the future." It was something to think about. Neither McKenzie or Max had considered that their choices could impact things in the future, or even people's lives. "Hey, don't you guys want to get some sleep tonight? Come on!"

The twins turned to look at one another. "Look," smiled Gina. "We're going back to bed. We'll talk about this over breakfast, okay?"

Max and McKenzie were disappointed, wanting to continue the conversation, but they didn't want to lose any time at Disney World the next day, so followed the suggestion their sister had made. "Okay," they shrugged.

Once they were alone again, Max asked, "Well, Kenz, what do you think? Are we going to continue with Curiel, or take a pass? I have to admit it is fascinating to go back to biblical times. It is so different than just reading about that time in history books. I vote we see this thing through."

"Me, too," agreed McKenzie, without hesitation. "Especially after what Colby said. I guess I just never thought I was important enough to make that much of a difference."

"I know. But we have to figure we would not have been asked if it was not important, even if we don't know the reason right now," added Max.

McKenzie chimed in. "That was so cool seeing that Dagon god, all smashed. And I learned much more than if I had just read about all that stuff. Yes, for sure I vote to continue."

It took a few moments for them to settle down, but the events of the day had worn them out, and they were asleep before five more minutes had elapsed.

CHAPTER 12

The jangling of the phone at 7:15 A. M. startled them. McKenzie picked it up and heard a voice that sounded a lot like Mickey Mouse advise her that she was receiving a wake-up call. She groaned, said thank you, and clambered out of bed and into the shower. Moments later she emerged from the bathroom, dressed and ready for the day, but saw that her twin brother hadn't stirred yet. She walked over to the door connecting the two rooms and tapped lightly.

Her sister opened the door and motioned her in. Her brother-in-law, like Max, was still sprawled across their bed, snoring. "Come on," whispered Gina. "We'll let them rack in a little."

The two young women tiptoed out of the room and made their way down to the Kona Cafe, where they each ordered Liliko'i juice, the specialty of the house, with passion fruit, orange and guava juices. Gina also ordered a cup of tea as they studied the menu.

"What're you doing today?" asked McKenzie.

"Meetings, starting at about 9:00," replied Gina with a little sigh. "Wish we had more time to tour the parks with you and Max. But what we are learning is valuable."

"We thought we might want to go to Epcot. Sorry you can't join us, but we would be happy to go on a ride for you," teased McKenzie. "That is, unless Max decides to stay in bed all day."

"Oh, wow, that makes me feel a whole lot better," laughed

Gina. "Well, Colby is still in the sack also."

"I suppose it's okay to relax on vacation, right?" McKenzie said.

"Yeah, sure," agreed Gina. "Colby's best friend, Jim Kane, came down here last Christmas with his wife and three kids. For five days in a row, he called the wake-up service so he and the family could get up at about 6:30 A. M. When he called for the sixth day, the operator said, 'Mr. Kane, can I ask you something?' 'Sure,' Jim said, feeling mystified. The operator asked, 'Aren't you on vacation?' 'Sure,' Jim said. 'Well,' said the operator, 'don't you think you might want to sleep in a couple of days?'"

Gina and McKenzie laughed. "Jim told us about it. He said that he and his wife talked it over, and woke up a couple of hours later the next few days."

The sisters chuckled at the story and ordered their Tonga toast breakfast. After seeing what it looked like when Max had it the day before, they decided it was a 'must try' item. By the time it arrived, Colby and Max had plopped down at the table. Colby was showered, shaved and looking bright and cheerful.

Gina looked at Max. " Good grief, Max, you look like you've been dragged backward through a privet hedge," she exclaimed, as he yawned and scratched his tummy. The group had a good laugh at his appearance, and he promised to go back to the room and take a shower after breakfast.

After some preliminary chat, the group engaged in some deeper conversation.

"What do you think you want to do about the challenge to keep looking for the Ark?" asked Colby.

"Well," said McKenzie. "It *is* scary to think about."

"I know," said Gina. "But look at it this way. We never knew our Great-Grandpa on Mom's side, remember?"

"That's true, yeah," said Max.

"I think he died pretty young," added McKenzie.

"Yes," said Gina. "But Mom told me something about it. He worked for the railroad, and was on his feet all day long. He was the chief steward on the dining car of the trains he served. In those days, train travel was pretty fancy. The dining car was more like a fine dining restaurant."

"Right," said Max. "I read about some of the great passenger trains in America in the 1920's and 1930's, like the Pennsylvania line and the New York Central."

"Well, when he retired, he was in pretty good condition," said Gina. "All that walking left him pretty fit. But after he retired, he stopped doing anything. It was as if he decided to retire from life."

"I remember," said Colby. "About all he did was go to the store with your great-grandmother in the late afternoon. Other than that, he read the paper, watched TV, and took it easy. He thought he was entitled to it."

"I don't know this story," said Max. "What happened?"

"He died when he was 72," said Colby. "It was a shame. He didn't get to see how well his grandchildren did in life, much less get to know his great-grandchildren."

"So what are you saying? We need to stay active?" suggested Max. "I don't think you need to worry about us. Kenz and I are really active, and I don't think we are facing retirement any time soon!"

"Well, yes, but that's only part of it," said Gina.

"I think what Gina is trying to say is that we also need

challenges in life," explained Colby. "We have to take on physical, mental and emotional challenges. We need to feel that our lives have meaning. Think about when Gina talked that couple into adopting that nice dog that her vet practice had taken in."

"Yeah," said Max, "I was there."

Gina gave him one of her warm and gentle smiles. "Of course you were," she said. "And you were part of that experience. That couple saw how well the dog related to you. Then she showed the same affection to the couple."

"A job well done," said Colby. "The point is, Gina's job is tough a lot of the time, but things like that make her feel that her life counts for something, do you see?"

"Sure," said the twins.

"Actually" explained McKenzie, "Max and I talked last night after you left the room and we both decided we want to participate in whatever it is Curiel wants us to do. Your story about Great Grandpa just confirms our decision, I think."

As the breakfast concluded the twins announced that they were going to spend the day at The Animal Kingdom. Colby and Gina left, each going to their respective meetings. Max went up to shower and change while McKenzie read the Orlando Sentinel newspaper. She liked to check out the comics in different newspapers.

When he returned, the twins tramped out to catch the bus to Animal Kingdom and walked around for a few hours, hitting a few of the rides and shows.

"We need to get to the Safari ride right away," announced McKenzie. "I was reading that the lines get really long pretty quick." Since it was on the other side of the entrance it took them a few minutes to get over there. They boarded their jeep after a fifteen minute wait and bounced around over the rough terrain, but they were rewarded with seeing most of the animals out and about. Their ride was even forced to come to a stop when a mama giraffe and her baby sauntered into the road and lingered there for a few minutes, allowing them to get some great pictures. They happened to get a great guide who was not only very knowledgeable about all the animals but also had a great sense of humor. About twenty-five minutes later they exited the ride and trying to decide what to do next.

"I know you wanted to see 'The Lion King' show," stated Max. "Do you want to go there next? I think the next show starts in about twenty minutes. It's just around the corner from here."

"Ooh, yes, let's do that. Everyone says it is 'THE BEST'!" And McKenzie took off at a fast clip.

"Okay then...." And Max found himself rushing to keep up. He found her in a short line near the ride waiting to get a picture with a photo shoot photographer. When she spotted him she motioned him him to join her.

"I thought you were in such a hurry," Max said.

"Well, it looks like we have some time before the doors open and I thought we should get a picture taken. Watch this next group. I think the pictures taken here have a fun cartoon animal that appears in the picture. You can tell because of the directions the photographer is giving the people," explained McKenzie.

Eventually they wandered over to the line just as everyone started to enter the Festival of the Lion King show. Within a few moments they were totally engaged in the high energy show. The thirty minutes of entertainment passed quickly and both of them chatted non-stop about how much fun it was as they were walking out of the theatre.

"What was your favorite part?" asked McKenzie. "I loved all the animal costumes and the wild dancing. Wouldn't it be fun to be in that show?"

Max agreed, "Well that was cool, but I think the best part was the monkeys. Their acrobatics were fantastic. Don't know about wanting to be in the show, though."

They continued their discussion of the pros and cons of being in a Disney show and soon found themselves standing at the entrance to Dinoland. Max spotted the Dino-Bite snack booth and insisted they grab some chips to tide them over. McKenzie sighed but willingly joined in the snacking. They strolled over to the ride called DINOSAUR, munching their recent purchase as they walked. Max, using a very theatrical voice, read from their guidebook. "DINOSAUR includes loud sounds in the dark and menacing dinosaurs that may be scary for children."

"I think we can handle it," teased his sister, giving him one of her looks.

The ride was remarkable in its lifelike animatronics, and Max and McKenzie laughed and screamed their way through it. As they came near the end, the car in which they were riding rolled toward a huge dinosaur that roared, showing its teeth and making menacing gestures. "I can see why they warn about little kids riding this thing," said Max. "That dino would be really scary for them."

"I know, " began McKenzie, but then a huge white light flashed around them and they found themselves standing in a desert, no longer in Florida.

"Curiel?" asked McKenzie, her voice trembling.

"Yes, McKenzie," said the warm, comfortable voice.

"We aren't back in the dinosaur era, are we?" asked McKenzie, a worried look skirting across her face.

Curiel laughed. "No, definitely not. This experience will give you an idea of the power of the Ark of the Covenant. You will be a witness and a participant in the defeat of Jericho under the command of Joshua." And then he vanished!

Max looked down and realized he was now wearing something resembling a short dress with a wide band around his waist. Attached to that and hanging at his side was a scabbard containing a battle sword.

"Whoa," cried McKenzie, "what are we wearing?" She too, was robed in similar garments. "And what do you have on your head?" Then she burst out laughing. "Where's my phone when I need it! This deserves a picture to post on Facebook."

"Ha! Ha!" said Max, shooting her a dirty look. He felt his head. "I am probably wearing the same thing you are. I think they are helmets of some kind. We seem to be dressed as soldiers. Are we going to have to fight in a war?" he asked with a nervous tremor in his voice. "I guess Curiel heard we were willing to go on an adventure," he added with resignation in his voice.

"Well, he certainly didn't waste any time before he called us here. Look, over there is what appears to be a temporary camp," McKenzie noticed, pointing. "And all those soldiers. There must be thousands of them!" Then she turned around. "Could that walled city over there be Jericho, the one Curiel just told us about?"

Just then a soldier approached from the direction of the camp. In a rough voice he scolded, "Come on, you two. Joshua has commanded all soldiers report for our last march around the town of Jericho. Where have you been? You should not wander away from the camp without letting us know. Go stand over there and follow instructions."

Without hesitation, Max and Kenzie obeyed the orders given by the soldier. They glanced sideways at each other, shrugged their shoulders, and hoped this was all part of Curiel's plan. They didn't dare to ask questions of the man as he seemed to think they should know exactly what he was talking about; but, in reality, they were very confused and very scared. Neither of them had ever been in a fight at school and they certainly had no idea how to use the weapon draped at their side.

As they walked into camp, everyone was excitedly chatting about the events of the last few days. No one seemed surprised to see them; in fact, they were greeted warmly. "Joash, Leticia, good to see you." They apparently were not only well known, but had names in this time and place. "We were just talking about how we have had to walk behind the priests and the Ark once a day, every day for the last six days, around the whole city of Jericho. What is your opinion of these strange orders our God has given to Joshua?" asked the man called Matthew.

The twins exchanged quick looks at one another. Thinking quickly, Max replied, "Well, I believe it is not my place to question as I am younger than many of you. Do you know why everyone is so excited?"

"Well, my young friend, you can hear for yourself what is about to happen. Look, here comes Joshua now with orders for today."

"Gather around. The time for rejoicing is near. Today is the day the Lord will deliver the city of Jericho into our hands," announced Joshua in a booming voice. "Today, as in the past six days, we will be led to march around the walls of Jericho by seven of our priests who will walk ahead of the Ark, followed by you soldiers. Each priest will carry a ram's horn. However, today we will march around the city seven times with the priests blowing their horns. When we have finished the priests will blow one final, very long blast on their horns. At this time the whole assembly will shout as loud as you are able. The walls of Jericho will then fall down and you will see the power of our great God who delivers us from our enemies in this city."

Everyone cheered and danced in anticipation and Max and McKenzie found themselves caught up in their enthusiasm as well. "This is going to be very exciting. Do you think we will be able to witness this entire event?" asked McKenzie.

"It sure seems like it," replied Max. "I have to say I am really happy it sounds like we don't have to use these weapons."

Joshua continued. "Assemble yourselves in the proper order and we shall begin our seven laps around the city as instructed by the Lord, our God." Immediately a group of armed soldiers moved to the front of the huge mob of people followed by the seven priests blowing their trumpets. Next came the priests in charge of carrying the Ark of the Covenant, and finally thousands of armed soldiers marching behind it.

Max and McKenzie held tightly to each other until the formations were completed so they would not lose track of one another. They found themselves in the middle of the assembled soldiers as they marched and both needed to focus until they got the rhythm of the marching steps accurate. They were taken by surprise at the precision of the march, especially considering the thousands of soldiers involved. "Are we going to be able to keep up with these men? They certainly keep a steady pace," noticed McKenzie. "I wish I had some water. I am really hot already."

"Just keep marching, Kenz. You will be fine. Look up there, on top of the wall," said Max, pointing. "All those people from Jericho are watching us and probably wondering what we are doing. This is amazing. I can't believe I am actually here participating in this event."

"Well, I feel like I have been tramping around these walls for ages," sighed McKenzie, sometime later. "But we are involved first hand in a part of ancient history. All those stories we've heard about for years are true and we are living one of them right this very minute!"

Suddenly the sound of a prolonged blast of the trumpets could be heard throughout the ranks of the marching men and as it finished, Max and Kenzie heard themselves shouting as loud as they were able along with thousands of other voices. At that instant they witnessed the miraculous.....the walls of the city collapsed all at once. Just as all the soldiers charged over the crumbled walls and into the town to capture it, the twins found themselves standing on the banks of the Jordan River with Curiel.

CHAPTER 13

"Did we really just see the destruction of Jericho?" asked Max, still in awe of their experience. "I mean all we did was walk around that city. Not one soldier even touched that wall. It just collapsed. If I hadn't seen it with my own eyes I don't think I would have believed it to be possible."

"You just witnessed an example of the importance of the Ark to the Hebrews, and the power of the Lord, their God." said Curiel.

"I get it," said McKenzie. "We're getting glimpses of how important the Ark would be today if it could be found and put back into the temple. I know I have heard about the Ark before but I had no idea it had so much power. I guess it makes sense that other people would want it recovered so they would have that power available as well."

"Well, now," said Curiel. "Do you believe that the power is in the Ark itself? That there is some magical power to it?"

"What do you mean?" asked McKenzie. "Didn't we just watch what it could do to the enemies of the Jewish people? I thought that's what you wanted us to see."

"Don't make the mistake of the Jewish nation when it went to war against the Philistines," said Curiel "Remember what you saw?"

"You mean when the Philistines captured the Ark," answered McKenzie.

"Yes, but where did that power come from?" persisted Curiel.

"I think I understand," said Max. "The Israelites were trusting that the Ark would save them from their enemies instead of trusting God. They were trusting that the symbol was where the power was and not God. It's almost like they were making the Ark the thing to be worshipped instead of their God who was supposed to be residing there so God let them lose the battle."

"Essentially, yes. There was a little more to it than that, but you are on the right track," said Curiel. Take some time to think through all you have seen. Now you must return to your sister and her husband. I will see you sometime soon. Perhaps you could spend a little time learning what you can about Solomon's temple, the later temples, and where people have looked for the Ark. The next time I come for you I may take you to the spot where it is hidden."

"We asked Gina and Colby about that," said Max. "But they don't know where the Hebrews hid the Ark and the other temple treasures."

"It is true," nodded Curiel. "No one alive remembers where they are hidden. But when the time comes the hiding place will be revealed."

Max and McKenzie began to comment on that information, but now they felt the familiar sensation of traveling through time and space. Soon they were back on the DINOSAUR ride in Disney's Animal Kingdom. The animatronic dinosaur looked pretty tame to them this time.

CHAPTER 14

The twins finished the DINOSAUR ride, somewhat sobered by what they had learned about the Ark of the Covenant. "Does this mean," asked Max, "that the Ark is probably not lost forever?"

"I think so," said McKenzie. "I wish we had a Bible expert to talk to, someone who really knows about Jewish Archeology."

"Agreed," said Max. "I don't know where we'd find such a person, though. It would mean a visit to the British Museum, or to one of the Universities, Oxford, Cambridge, or something."

"The problem with that, of course," said McKenzie, "is that we haven't a shred of proof that we've had any adventures with ancient Israel, right?"

"No, we don't," shrugged Max. "And how can we do that while we are in DisneyWorld?"

"Let's ask Curiel," she suggested.

"How do we call him?" he asked. "He's always been here when we've traveled through the Amulet."

"It's true," she said. "But didn't he tell us to relax for a bit when we got back?"

"Yeah, I guess he did," Max agreed. "But this is pretty important, wouldn't you say?"

"Sure it is, but let's do what he advised and have a little fun. It will also give us time to think about what we have seen and heard. And somehow, I kind of think that he will see we get the information we need when we actually need it. He has supplied us we all the knowledge we have needed so far. I don't think we should worry about it too much. So, now, what do you want to do next?"

"How about the Kali River Rapids? I really like the water rides and we haven't done one yet."

"Sounds fun," agreed McKenzie. "It's certainly warm enough and looks like it's not too far from where we are."

So they quickly headed over to the Asia area and stepped in line. Soon they were climbing into the circular raft. As they settled into their seats they couldn't help but notice that all the other people were wearing water ponchos. "So do you think we will get really wet on this ride," Kenzie asked the others who were busy securing their seat belts.

They all laughed. "You bet," one man responded. "It's a blast, but you guys better prepare to be soaked by the time it's over."

Kenzie groaned. "Oh, well, I guess it's only water. And in this weather we should dry off in no time," replied Max.

The man was right. After howling and laughing their way through the tumultuous ride, they exited the raft with very little of their clothing, or hair, that was not drenched in water. They decided to walk around the Maharajah Jungle Trek in hopes their clothes would dry out a little. They stopped to watch the Flights of Wonder show which turned out to be much more entertaining than expected.

"You know, I am still completely wet," complained McKenzie. "It's too bad we didn't have ponchos cause I am pretty uncomfortable. Do you think we can go back to the room so I can change clothes?"

"Sure, I guess so," replied Max. "Maybe we can grab something to eat, too."

They wove their way back to the entrance and hopped on a bus back to the Polynesian. "Why don't we hang around at the pool this afternoon after we grab something to tide us over until dinner," suggested McKenzie. "It's already 2 P.M. and by the time we change, eat, and go to a park it will almost be time to return and meet Gina and Colby."

"Sounds like a plan," agreed Max.

Returning to their room, they changed into their swimsuits. Max threw on a t-shirt while McKenzie pulled a cover-up over her head. They stopped at Captain Cook's, the counter service restaurant, and ordered an Hawaiian flatbread to share. On the way out, they each grabbed a brownie and a bottle of water before walking out to the pool.

"How about setting up our lounge chairs over there on the sand," suggested McKenzie. "It will be a little quieter and I can listen to my book on my Kindle."

"Yeah, that's a good idea. I wonder when we'll see Curiel again. I am kind of looking forward to these adventures," said Max.

They carted all their stuff over to the beach area and settled into their chairs, munching on the brownies they had brought with them, each enjoying their reading material. It was not long, however, before they hard a familiar voice.

"Patience," said a voice behind them. The twins turned to see a tall, thin man in swim trunks, a t-shirt, and red crocs approach. "Dear twins, I am so glad to see you."

"Curiel, is that you?" screeched McKenzie, laughing so hard she had to hold her stomach. "We've never seen you dressed like this."

Max, too, stood laughing with hopeless desperation.

Somehow seeing the angel dressed as a modern man ready for the swimming pool felt totally weird. "We're sorry, Curiel, but those clothes just seem so out of character for you," explained Max.

"No offense taken. Are these not the proper clothes for a pool? I did not want to draw attention to myself so thought it appropriate to attempt to fit in."

"Well, I think you did a magnificent job fitting in," declared Kenzie, trying to muffle another giggle.

Curiel smiled. "Come, I think you are ready for your next lesson."

He instructed them to hold up their amulets. They obeyed, and the air began to swirl around them.

"Where are we now?" asked McKenzie.

"The mountain where Jesus was crucified," said the Angel, and the twins exchanged glances. They thought that they heard a sadness in his voice. Can angels cry, thought Max. "Yes, we can," said Curiel, with a smile.

"Yes, you can what?" asked McKenzie.

"Cry," said Curiel. "Your brother thought the question to me."

"I believe Curiel can listen to our thoughts," explained Max.

"Is that true?" asked McKenzie, turning back to the Angel.

"Of course," explained Curiel. "If I am going to help you, I need to know what is troubling you. Didn't you notice I appeared at the beach after Max mentioned his desire for another adventure?"

"Yes, that's right," said McKenzie. "We thought you weren't there. We believed we were all by ourselves a few moments ago."

"No, not alone," said Curiel. "We were with you and had you near to us. You are never completely by yourselves. If we would leave you, you would be without protection."

"No thanks," said Max, with a great deal of emphasis.

"Do not be afraid," said Curiel. "You will always have the protection of the Eternal. So, now, are you ready for the adventure I have planned for you?" asked the Angel.

The twins looked at one another, then back at their friend, and said in unison, "Yes."

CHAPTER 15

The swirling motion subsided, having transported them to their new location.

"Now where is Curiel?" asked Max, looking all around at the unfamiliar surroundings. "I thought he was here with us." When he looked up he saw a man in in a wide-brimmed hat, long pants, heavy duty shoes, and sunglasses walking toward them.

"I don't know," confessed McKenzie, "he seems to have the disturbing habit of disappearing without warning, but judging from what this guy is wearing, I don't think we are back in ancient times. I do wish Curiel wouldn't leave us so suddenly without any directions."

Max continued her thoughts, "I know, but at least he has left us in the same place. The mountain is still right here. It's just that Curiel is not!"

"Hey, there," said the man. "I'm so glad you could come to join us. If you had given us your exact travel information we would have arranged for transportation from the airport over here. When did you get in? Well, never mind, I'm just glad to see you. We can really use your help. Oh, by the way, I'm Ron Wyatt. You must be McKenzie and Max. I read your application and resume, very impressive indeed for your age. Well, let's get a move on and I'll fill you in on all the excitement around here."

"How do you do, sir," greeted Max, and both he and Kenzie shook hands with him. Glancing at one another with a quizzical look, both wondered how he received an application neither had filled out! At this point, again they were thoroughly confused but had learned to hope their mission would soon become clear.

"I know that I was a little vague about what you would be doing here but we have to keep this somewhat quiet until we achieve our purpose. Let me explain," began Ron. "What we are doing here is ground-breaking. We are searching for the lost Ark of the Covenant, and we strongly believe we are in the general area of its location."

"Are you an archeologist, sir?" asked McKenzie.

Ron laughed a little. "Well, not exactly," he said. "At least, not by training. An amateur, I am afraid, who has devoted much of his life to the study of biblical archeology. And I have found some pretty neat stuff. I was able to discover the land bridge across the Red Sea, connecting Egypt with what is now Arabia. It was there that we found the artifacts related to the crossing of the nation of Israel, artifacts from the exodus of Israel from Egypt."

"B-b-but then..." said Max. "You must have met our friends, Marina and Dan," he said, stumbling on his words of amazement..

"Yes, indeed," Ron said, grinning.

"Oh, wow, this is fabulous," exclaimed McKenzie, now becoming very interested in this new adventure. "And we are going to be allowed to assist in the discovery?"

"That is the idea, yes. We are counting on your help. When the Babylonians captured Jerusalem, a very detailed list of items taken from the temple to Babylon never mentioned the Ark and it also was never a part of the returned items. Based on all of my research, I feel it was hidden somewhere right around here."

"So have you started digging? Have you found anything yet?" asked Max.

"Well, yes, with the help of my sons, Danny and Ronny. We began our search for biblical treasures back in 1978 when we were diving in the Red Sea. At that time I was strongly motivated to dig in a very specific spot for the Ark so we have come back to continue looking for it."

By now we had walked to an area where a huge rock was sitting. There was also a large stone extending out from the cliff face just above it. Standing next to the rock were two men.

"Oh, here are my boys. Ronny, Danny, I want you to meet our new helpers, Max and McKenzie," said Ron.

"Boy, are you two a sight for sore eyes," said Ronny.

"And for sore muscles," added Danny, laughing. "We were really looking forward to your arrival. I hope we are able to make an exciting discovery while you are here."

Ronny continued, "We think this rock is pretty unusual and too symmetrical to be here accidentally. What do you say we try to move it? I think if we all help we can examine it more closely."

"Yes," explained Ron. "It seems to have a coating of travertine on it which is most unusual."

"What, exactly, is travertine and why is that of importance?" questioned McKenzie.

""Well, today it is used as a tile for floors or walls," explained Ron. "Travertine is a form of limestone deposited by mineral springs, especially hot springs. It is formed when the underground mineral water seeps through limestone, dissolving it and in this case, it was redeposited in the form of a coating on this rock."

Max was trying to understand. "So you don't think this rock was here naturally, but that it was deliberately placed here."

"That would seem to be the case, yes," said Danny.

"Then let's get busy moving it," said McKenzie, anxious to begin.

All five of them got behind the boulder and pushed and shoved until it gave way. Once it was moved they discovered a hole that had been hammered or chiseled into the rock.

"Okay, let's start excavating here," ordered Ron.

"Gosh, what do you think is down that hole?" asked Max.

"Let's find out," said Ronny, grabbing his tools.

They dug for quite a while, removing mounds of dirt and stones until they discovered a shelf like structure with twelve inch square hole in the center. Soon they uncovered two more platforms, or shelf structures,, each with the same type of holes in the center. One was raised up higher than the others.

Ron indicated they should stop. "Do you realize what we are probably looking at," exclaimed Ron with obvious excitement in his voice.

They all glanced at him. Max and Kenzie shrugged their shoulders and waited for the explanation.

"I believe we have uncovered the location of the crucifixion of Jesus. Look, those holes were where the crosses would have been placed, and the elevated platform was for the cross of Jesus. I can't prove this, of course, but it certainly fits," suggested Ron.

"And look," noticed Max, "there is a huge crack in the center platform, the one that is higher than all the others. It extends all the way up into the rock around it."

"Dad, doesn't the Bible talk about an earthquake at the

moment that Jesus died?" asked Danny.

"Yes, it does," said Ron. "I have a small New Testament in my jacket pocket. Let me go get it."

"So we could really be looking at the place where Jesus was crucified?" asked McKenzie. "Does that mean that we are digging in the right place to find the Ark?"

"If what Dad believes is correct," said Ronny. "His theory is that the blood of Jesus would have seeped down through the cracks in the rocks and fallen on the Ark of the Covenant hidden many years before.

Ron returned, flipping the pages of the little testament. He looked up and said, "Here is the passage: this is from the Gospel of of Matthew, Chapter 27. It says: 'And when Jesus had cried out again in a loud voice, he gave up his spirit. At that moment the curtain of the temple was torn in two from top to bottom. The earth shook, the rocks split and the tombs broke open.' It certainly seems to be saying that there was an earthquake."

"Well, this looks like evidence of an earthquake, doesn't it?" observed Max.

"Just keep digging and if you find an object, carefully remove it and set it aside to be cleaned and labeled," explained Ron patiently.

The twins worked without ceasing, only stopping for water breaks, until it was time to eat. Mr. Wyatt had brought food for them and they sat around a fire eating while going over the day's events. "We will spend the night here just to be safe. People may be too curious about what we are doing here and try to sabotage our work or continue it without us," explained Ron. They turned in early, just at sundown, and fell asleep in their sleeping bags immediately, exhausted from all the hard work of the day.

In the next few days they continued helping with the archeological dig. Lunchtime arrived on the fourth day, and the twins decided to take a short walk around the area to explore a little.

"Just think, Kenz, we could be involved in the making of history," declared Max.

"I know, I know," said McKenzie. "I just hope our efforts prove to be worthwhile, especially for Mr. Wyatt. He has put so much of himself into this search and would be so disappointed if we didn't find the Ark. Just think, we could be the first people in centuries to see it."

Without any warning the twins felt the familiar sensation of swirling air and were again sitting on the sandy beach in lounge chairs at the the Polynesian Hotel.

They stared at each other and began talking at once.

"What? Oh no!" squealed McKenzie. "I mean were we actually digging to help discover the Ark. Why couldn't we stay and finish?How many days were we digging and sorting artifacts anyway?"

Max checked his watch. With a look of disbelief on his face he announced, "It appears that, again, no time has passed unless we returned at the exact time we left, only days later."

"How can that be? My arms actually ache from all that digging and I am sure we slept there a few nights in sleeping bags."

"Beats me," said Max. "But I believe anything is possible with Curiel in charge."

"That man we met, Ron Wyatt, wasn't he inspiring?" continued McKenzie. "He was so convinced that he was supposed to be over in Israel searching for the Ark. There was no hesitation in his belief about his mission, was there?"

"His dedication to the project impressed me. I mean he used all of his own money and resources to follow what his heart was telling him. This is one adventure I will never forget. I only wish we had been there to see the discovery of the Ark. Can you imagine what would be like?" said Max, disappointment evident in his voice.

"Yea, I know," sighed McKenzie.

As they were reviewing their time with Ron Wyatt, they were aware of a man pulling a chair up right next to them. He sat down in his chair, his flashy, bright colored swim trunks catching their attention. When they glanced over towards the man, McKenzie screamed, "Curiel, where did you go? We had the most amazing adventure just now. We helped a man named Ron Wyatt in his search for the missing Arc. Do you think he will find it? Why didn't we get to stay longer?" She continued to bombard him with questions until he had to interrupt her.

Curiel smiled. "Haven't I warned you about being patient, beloved? I am glad you found this assignment to be of interest. In due time your questions will be answered. Did you learn anything while there?"

She pouted, and gave a sly, sideways look. "Well, I guess I am learning patience!"

This remark caused both Curiel and Max to laugh. "True enough," agreed Max.

"You must remember that there will be a proper time for the presence of the Ark to be revealed to the world. What might be the danger of it appearing at the wrong time?"

"People could try to use it for their own purposes, which

could be for evil," said Max.

"It could start a war if lots of countries claimed it or stole it," added McKenzie.

"Or people might dishonor God by thinking that owning it gives them special powers like the Philistines. Even the Jews acted like that at times," reasoned Max.

"I am proud of you both," commented Curiel. "You have learned much and Max, I notice that you have not stuttered for quite awhile. Perhaps you have grown more confident?"

McKenzie chimed in. "I hadn't even noticed, Max, but that is so true."

"You know," added Max, "that is one of the best things that has ever happened for me!"

"I must leave now," announced Curiel. "I believe you are due to meet your sister and Colby for dinner shortly." And in the next instant he was gone.

The twins splashed around in the pool and then decided to go down the water slide a few times. Soon they checked the time and saw it was time to go back to their room to get cleaned up and changed for dinner.

As they were placing their magic bands on their wrists McKenzie asked, "Hey, Max, do you remember where we are supposed to meet for dinner? Are we just going to a restaurant here at the hotel?"

"I think Colby said something about the 'Wave', didn't he?"

"Oh, boy, I hope we aren't going to be late. Let's stop at the front desk and find out where that is."

They closed up the room and discovered that they needed to hop on the monorail since the restaurant, 'The Wave...of American Flavors', was located in the Contemporary Resort.

"I guess we should have paid more attention to the details of where we were going," admitted McKenzie.

"We'll be fine. Just be glad we weren't supposed to eat somewhere that isn't on the monorail. Then we would be in a tight spot. As it is we will only be a couple minutes late."

The twins entered the Contemporary and found the restaurant without difficulty after asking directions. They found Colby and Gina in the Lounge area waiting for them and were promptly seated.

"I am starving," announced Max.

"You are always starving," added McKenzie.

"Well, then," said Colby, "let's get some appetizers, shall we?"

The waitress arrived and took their orders. "Now that we have taken care of the essentials," laughed Gina, "can you tell me if you guys have had a fun day?"

The twins exploded in their enthusiasm to share the events of the day. They struggled to get everything out without interrupting one another. It took the entire dinner to complete their story. Colby and Gina listened intently and once they stopped talking for a few moments, Colby took the opportunity to clarify what he had heard, "So you have had a few pretty unique and exciting adventures. You really were with a guy helping him dig for the lost Ark of the Covenant? I have to say that is the most extraordinary news I have heard in a long time."

"Well, I think that this calls for a dessert order in celebration of your very special adventure," announced Gina. "How about we order a couple of the dessert flights to share?"

"Oooh, yes! Can we get the chocolate one?" suggested Kenzie.

"Sure, we'll get a couple of them," agreed Colby.

They motioned to their waitress and placed their dessert order. It came quickly and they lingered over it, continuing with additional details of their time with Ron Wyatt. "I can understand why you are upset you weren't able to remain and see how the search turned out. Did Curiel tell you if you would be able to go back and continue to help?" asked Gina?

"Well, I hope so, but there were no guarantees made," admitted Max.

It was close to 8:30 by the time they left the restaurant so Colby suggested they go see the light show and fireworks over in the Magic Kingdom since they were so close to it. Everyone, except Max, agreed that this was a great idea. "Isn't that just for little kids?" he asked. "Besides we already saw fireworks from the Grand Floridian." He was outvoted and so trailed along with the others. The monorail was just pulling in as they arrived in the lobby so they all hopped on and then hustled through the crowd in the park to find a spot in front of the castle.

McKenzie was quite impressed. "This is just beautiful. I am so glad we came over to watch this show. Look at the colors on the castle. I love the greens and blues, but it's now pink, and look, now it's changing again!" She glanced over to Max. "You have to admit this is pretty cool."

"Yea, I guess I'm glad we came," he said. "It is pretty neat. I really liked the music video stuff."

Once the fireworks ended, Colby encouraged them to get to the side quickly and walk briskly to avoid the crowds pushing to get to the exit and the transportation back to their hotels. They were able to catch the monorail back to the Polynesian within a short time. Gina informed them that she and Colby would be getting up early to eat breakfast. The twins, exhausted after their exciting day, announced that they should not plan on them in the morning. "I think we will probably sleep in tomorrow," said Max, looking to Kenzie for confirmation. She nodded her head in agreement and plodded into their bedroom where she grabbed her pajamas, and whisked into the bathroom to change. Within a few minutes, both twins were in their beds checking their messages before falling asleep.

The next morning Kenzie awoke and checked the time: 9:30! "Hey, Max, wake up. We're missing the whole day!"

"Huh?" mumbled Max. "Kenz, it's probably only about 6. Go back to sleep."

In response McKenzie whipped open the curtains and bright sunlight streamed into the room. "I don't think so," she bellowed. Then, she started singing a silly wake-up song their mom used to sing to get them out of bed, when they were young.

"Ok. Ok. I'm up. I'm up," he insisted. "Just stop singing 'Birdie with a Yellow Bill'!" While he was continuing to wake up, she showered and changed and then he took his turn in the bathroom.

"Let's just stop at the quick service and grab something to eat on the way out," said Max.

"That's a great idea." So they stopped at Captain Cook's, filled their mugs, and chose a few doughnuts to munch as they traveled. "Are we going to Epcot today?"

"Yea, I thought that's what we decided last night", confirmed Max.

They climbed onto the bus to transport them to the park and took a seat away from others near the rear. Once seated,

McKenzie took out her amulet to look at it. "Max, do you think we will have an adventure today? I mean with Curiel?"

Before he could answer, they both felt the familiar swirling motion. They were transported into a desert type landscape similar to what they experienced previously. They immediately saw a friendly and familiar figure.

"Beloved, today you have come to a mountain called Carmel," announced Curiel. "It is some distance from Jerusalem. It was, years ago, a hideout for criminals because it has thick vegetation on the sloped hillside, and several caves on the steeper side. As a haunt for criminals, they believed it offered an escape from God. "

"Can people really escape from God?" asked McKenzie, sounding surprised.

"Of course not," said Curiel. "But this is how it was seen: a place of safety for criminals."

"A hide-out," said Max. "So what is going on here, Curiel?"

"King Ahab has led the Israelites into the worship of the false God, Baal, so Elijah, the Jewish prophet, has called all the other prophets serving Baal, along with the king and all the people, to this mountain to settle the matter once and for all as to who is the true God. Now listen as Elijah addresses this group," said Curiel. "They are unable to see us. Just listen and learn."

Elijah began, "I am the only prophet of the Lord here, but there are four hundred fifty prophets of Baal. Bring two bulls. Let the prophets of Baal choose one bull, kill it and cut it into pieces. Then let them put the meat on the wood, but they are not to set fire to it. I will prepare the other bull, putting the meat on the wood I assemble but not setting fire to it. You prophets of

Baal, pray to your god, and I will pray to the Lord. The god who answers by setting fire to his wood is the true God." All the people agreed to this solution.

As the twins watched, the prophets of Ball prepared a pile their pile of wood and Elijah prepared his pile. The prophets of Baal were the first to attempt to get their god to light the fire. From morning to noon these prophets begged their god to start a fire while dancing around the pile of logs. Exhausted, they finally slowed down. Then the twins spotted a tall, gray-haired man standing in front of the other pile of rocks. Now they could hear Elijah taunting the other priests.

As they listened, they could hear the man yelling insults: "Louder!" Elijah yelled. "Maybe Baal is asleep, or on a trip, or in the toilet!"

Max and McKenzie couldn't help laughing at the thought of the cow-headed creature they called a god using a public washroom. Still the priests of Baal continued their pleas.

Finally, Elijah called out to the crowd. "Come here to me, friends." He directed the attention of the crowd to the slaughtered animal near his improvised altar. He and his assistants lifted the cow's carcass onto the stack of wood that Elijah and his men had piled onto his altar. "Bring the water!" yelled Elijah.

The men poured water from enormous water jugs onto the carcass and the wood. Then the men poured another flood of water. And again. The altar, the wood, and the carcass were soaked with water. When the altar and the sacrifice, as well as the surrounding ground, was pooled with water, he lifted his head and prayed. He asked that God would show that he was the true God, and that he'd done these things.

The prayer lasted less than a minute. The sky turned a bright orange and fire streamed down from the sky creating a gigantic blaze as the teenagers watched. The sacrifice was burned, as were the wood, stones, and the soil. The water around the altar vanished also, and in moments, all that was left was a smoking pile of ashes. Not a speck of the original sacrifice remained. Max and McKenzie's eyes widened and they stepped back as Curiel grabbed their hands to reassure them. Both were amazed and somewhat shaken at the awesome power displayed by the event they just witnessed.

Now the fire plummeted down on the pagan altar. Max and McKenzie's jaws dropped as the pagan altar and sacrifice was also reduced to a pile of ashes in a matter of moments. All the people gathered around gasped in unison at the sight caused by the destruction of fire shooting down from the skies above them.

"Come, Beloved," said Curiel. And the familiar swirl of air began, and the twins were now standing on a plain, looking at a red sky and a colorful sunset.

"Why did you bring us to see that, Curiel?" wondered McKenzie.

"I think I might know," offered Max. "It is to show us that the true God, the God of Israel, is all powerful. That his power is independent of the Ark so we have no doubt about what we learned earlier when others thought that just by owning the ark they owned God's power."

"Also, the people saw that what they had chosen to believe was a lie," added McKenzie.

"Yes, it appeared as completely false," said the Angel. "They had rejected worship of the true God and selected Baal, an abominable monster god, as the center of their lives. When they had to deal with the consequences of turning away from God, they began to turn to Baal instead of repenting and asking for forgiveness. The pagan god was a falsehood. They exchanged the truth for a lie. And although we did not remain to see this, the people hated Elijah, whom God had chosen, and did not treat him well," said Curiel. "People do not like to be confronted with their sin."

"You mean they don't like hearing the truth," said McKenzie.

"I think your time here has proved effective. See that you both remember these lessons. But come," said Curiel. "I must return you to your home. No, do not protest. I will see you soon."

"What is soon?" asked Max, and he felt, as always, the profound sadness of saying good-bye to a dear friend. Curiel was more than a friend, he knew.

"Every time is 'soon'," smiled Curiel.

The twins stood and hugged their friend. "Keep the amulets safe, Beloved ones," said the Angel.

In the next moment, the twins were standing at Epcot and proceeded to the turnstiles, pressing their magic bands against the Mickey face to gain entrance. They were quiet as they walked toward Spaceship Earth, both deep in thought over their recent experience. Finally, McKenzie commented, "Do you think we will see Curiel again?"

Max took his time in responding, "I do, but for some reason I don't think it will be real soon. He told us to keep our amulets; he didn't tell us to give them to anyone else."

"That's true," agreed McKenzie. "Maybe we have to take some time to fully absorb all the things we saw and did. I mean, we have seen the Ark, Elijah, the capture of the Ark, all kinds of things. No one else living today has had the opportunities we just had."

"Makes me feel stupid for worrying about my popularity or my stutter," continued Max. "That is not what we are to focus on, is it?"

"No, it isn't. I think we need to really investigate what our personal faith really means to us. How can we question the reality of God and his power ever again? I think we have been given a very special gift in these adventures," added Kenzie.

CHAPTER 16

A year passed quickly and the twins had no adventures. Still, they did not waste their time. They researched the Lore of the Ark of the Covenant, and talked to archeologists. Gina and Colby had made friends with a man who was the head of a missionary organization and they took McKenzie and Max to meet him while he was in town giving a lecture series in a nearby church.

Dr. Jeff Johnson and his wife, Louise, headed a group called Israel Today, which was headquartered in the Dallas, Texas area. Gina and Colby asked them to dinner and the twins were included in the invitation. They took this opportunity to ask what Jeff and Louise thought of the search for the Lost Ark. "I think that the temple could be re-built," said Jeff, "without the Ark of the Covenant and the rest of the temple treasures. But if they could be found and included in the consecration, it would be a huge blessing for the Israeli people."

Max and McKenzie spent the next couple hours relating their time spent with Ron Wyatt searching for the Lost Ark and answering many questions. The twins were a little worried that the pastor and his wife might scoff at their story, or think they were making it up, but they both listened intently.

"I don't quite know what to say. I know many people have searched for these treasures in recent years with little success. That God intervened in your life and gave you such an amazing opportunity is truly special," said Pastor Johnson. "People have considered the Ark and its whereabouts for almost three thousand years. Perhaps you will be blessed with a continuation of these adventures. It seems you will have to wait and see what the future holds. In the meantime I will keep monitoring news reports about any events relating to this very topic." He gave them both an encouraging smile.

CHAPTER 17

The school year was winding up in a couple weeks and the twins sat together at the dining room table one night, trying to decide on what do for the summer.

"Maybe I could be a lifeguard or work at a youth camp," said McKenzie.

"I guess I could volunteer to help the coaches with the freshmen football camp," said Max. "That would be fun, but wouldn't get me any money. I really would like to earn a few bucks this summer. One of my friends is going to be painting houses. I guess I could ask if he could put in a good word for me, but I have to admit I can't drum up much excitement over the prospect of scraping off paint in the heat. I guess I would do it, though."

"Do you want fun or do you want money in your pocket?" teased Kenzie. "Maybe Gina could use some help at the vet's office."

Max gave her one of his looks and replied, "Oh, yeah, cleaning dog poop out of the back area sounds almost as much fun as getting up on a ladder painting houses." At this comment they both started to laugh.

"Maybe we could go to Orlando and get a job at Disney World," suggested Kenz.

"Oh, yeah, that would get over really well with Mom and Dad," replied Max.

They continued this discussion about summer job choices for

awhile and Max noticed his sister was wearing her amulet. She still wore it most of the time, always hoping they would be called to complete their adventure with the Ark. The reflection of the dining room light on the medallion was unusual and he kept staring at it. Then, without warning, the amulet began flashing...

"Kenz!" he cried. "The amulet!" He jumped to his feet and ran to his room. He pulled his amulet from his bedside table and saw that it was turning into a picture. He covered it with his hand and ran back to the dining room. To his surprise, he saw that his sister was holding up her amulet and a swirling cloud had begun to emerge from the jewelry. It expanded to enfold Kenz. He dove at the cloud...

CHAPTER 18

Max felt himself spiraling out of control into a vortex of swirling lights, tornado-like winds, unimaginable sounds and… "Music?" he thought. Yes. It had to be. It was unlike any music he'd ever heard, however. It was much purer, clearer, and soft, but loud enough to be heard.

Then it stopped. He found himself standing in what? A hospital room?

Sure, that's what it was. It had the antiseptic smell of medicine and illness.

"McKenzie?" he whispered.

"Yeah, Max," said his sister, coming to stand at his side. She took his arm.

"Why are we in a hospital?" he asked.

"Visiting someone sick, I think," said McKenzie.

"Yes, you're correct," said a familiar voice.

"Curiel," they said, speaking in quiet, hushed voices, but surprised to see him in this setting.

"Yes, Beloved."

"What are we doing here?" asked McKenzie, as the twins hugged their Angel friend.

"You are correct. This is a hospital and I want you to see who's here. He wants to tell you something," smiled Curiel. The twins exchanged glances.

"Why?" they asked in unison. "Who? Have we met him before?"

"Yes, I believe you have," said their friend, with a twinkle in his eyes. "Come," he said.

The angel put his arms around the twins and walked with them over to the bed. The man in the bed struggled to open his eyes and look at them.

The twins gazed at the man with instant recognition. The questions came tumbling out in their excitement at seeing their friend again, "Mr. Wyatt, what is wrong? Why are you here in this hospital? What happened with your search for the Ark?"

"I'm sorry, Max and McKenzie," Mr. Wyatt managed. "I am afraid I am unable to continue with the recovery of the Ark. I have made my last trip there."

The twins were heartbroken at this news and upset that their friend was so sick that he would not be able to continue with his lifelong mission.

"Will you please tell them about finding the Ark?" said Curiel.

"What?" said the twins in unison. "You found the Ark of the Covenant?!"

Ron nodded. "Yes," he smiled. "I never could go back to retrieve it, though I tried and tried."

"Please, Ron," said Curiel. "You must tell them now."

"Of course," said Ron. "Here's what you two must do." For the next several minutes, he gave them directions on how to locate the Ark.

"Us? You want us to go without you? How will we ever be able to do that?" asked Max, sounding exasperated at the thought.

Curiel spoke up. "Have you not learned anything about faith during your past adventures? Perhaps I misjudged you." The sternness of Curiel's comment hit home. It had the desired effect.

"I'm sorry, of course you're right. Go ahead, Ron. We are listening, right, Kenz?"

Kenzie nodded her head, not able to speak, her stomach churning in anticipation of what she was about to hear. It is one thing to know what you must do, but it is altogether another thing to go boldly forward without hesitation in obedience.

"You must be careful," he cautioned. "This is located in what is now hostile territory. You will need to watch out and remain alert for dangers you would not normally encounter. From your previous time with me, you have enough knowledge to complete the task. Please be careful."

"Do you fully understand the mission you are about to accomplish?" questioned Curiel.

Though somewhat overwhelmed by the task they were facing, both nodded their heads in agreement. "So you won't be coming with us then?" asked a shaken McKenzie.

"You must know you will be under my watchful eye the entire time," encouraged Curiel. "I have great confidence in both of you."

CHAPTER 19

Within moments they found themselves in a foggy, quiet area like a swamp. The ground was wet, but to their surprise, their clothes and shoes remained dry. "Where did we land?" asked McKenzie.

"I don't have a clue," said Max. "It's warm, and foggy, like inside a cloud."

"Yeah," said McKenzie, taking in her surroundings.

They continued walking and soon noticed that the fog had begun to lift. "Is it just me, or is it getting brighter?" she wondered aloud.

"Yes," said Max. "I think the fog is beginning to lift."

"Well, one good thing," shrugged McKenzie. "We can't be in a Vampire movie."

They both began to giggle, but found themselves getting sober and even somewhat sad? "True," agreed Colby. "Ron was a nice man, wasn't he? I get the impression we won't see him again."

"I think you are right about that. He looked really sick," said McKenzie. "A brave man, and so committed without concern for himself."

They walked in silence for some time, and were soon standing in front of a strange, but familiar mountain. "We've been here," announced McKenzie. The sun was out now, and a bright light was shining on the mountain. "A couple years ago."

Max snapped his fingers. "Yeah, of course," he smiled. "It's the Place of the Skull."

McKenzie's mind had been somewhat fogged, but now it cleared also. "Calvary!" she cried. "Curiel brought us here. We saw inside this mountain, too. We saw."

"The blood," he remembered.

Without hesitation, McKenzie held up her amulet. The surface of it swirled, and it expanded around them, taking them to another location.

CHAPTER 20

Now they recognized their surroundings. They knew that they were inside the mountain, transported by the amulet.

"Over there," announced Max. He pointed to a brownish red stain on the top of a rock and said, "That's it, Kenz," he said, almost too excited to stand still. "I think that's the bloodstain."

"Oh my gosh," said his sister. "It's true, then. This blood dripped down here from the cross, didn't it."

"Well, we can't prove it," said Max. "But I remember Ron said he believed that to be true."

"And this must be it," said McKenzie, almost paralyzed by the implications of what they were viewing. "Oh my gosh. This is an amazing honor to be here, isn't it?"

"It's more than that," said Max. "If Ron was right, the blood also dripped on the Ark of the Covenant."

"Start looking," encouraged McKenzie. "We might be very close."

"Right," agreed her brother. They crawled around the small cavern on their hands and knees. After several minutes, they found a hole. It was about three feet across, and it looked forbidding and deep.

"Dark," mumbled McKenzie, her voice trembling a little.

"I'll say," said Max. "Do we go down there?"

McKenzie was silent. After a few moments, she confessed, "I'm scared. We don't have any idea what could be down there. Yucky spiders or snakes." A shiver ran through her body at the thought. She had always despised spiders and snakes. "Or it might cave in on us and we could be smothered!"

"I know," said her brother, understanding her fears were real. "I can go. You wait here."

"Aren't you scared too?" she asked.

"Yeah," he admitted. "But I'm just going to have to do it scared. I have to follow this thing through."

"What?" she said, now feeling a little ashamed.

"Sometimes you have to do things that scare you," shrugged Max. "So you just go ahead and do them scared."

"I guess so," said his sister with reluctance. "I suppose that the only way I will be able to get better at confronting what I am afraid of is by facing up to it. Just moving forward and doing it, right?"

"Gina reminded me of a story the other day," he continued. "We were talking about when she decided to apply to Veterinarian college. She didn't know if she was a good enough student."

"Gina?" gasped McKenzie. "She's a great student."

"Of course she is," noted Max. "Colby told her not to be silly. He also said that no matter what happened, he'd love her anyway."

"Yeah," said McKenzie. "Anyone can see how he feels about her."

"And that was what did the trick," said Max. "She knew that whatever happened, she had a solid base of support from people who loved her."

"Right," said McKenzie, her eyebrows squeezed together indicating she was deep in thought.

She was silent. "Okay, how do we get down there?"

"We?" he grinned.

"Yeah, of course," she said, and punched his arm. "You don't think I'm going to let you face those nasty spiders and snakes alone, do you?"

Then they heard a familiar voice, "Use the amulets."

CHAPTER 21

Together, the twins immediately held up their amulets and a new, unknown scene appeared. It was apparently a garage, for they saw ropes, hooks and safety belts. They stepped through.

"Now what is this?" whispered McKenzie. She looked around the room and felt somewhat nervous. No one seemed to be around.

"I haven't any idea," said Max. "But I don't think that we're going to get in trouble if we just borrow some stuff, will we? This looks like exactly what we need for the assignment we have been given."

Kenzie smirked. "Leave it to Curiel to anticipate our needs."

She lifted a coil of rope, then an adjustable climbing belt. Max did the same. "Ready?" he asked. She held up her amulet, and she reappeared in the cave. Max grabbed a couple of flashlights, two pairs of leather gloves, and a couple of other items he thought might come in handy. Holding the gear, he stepped into the light as well. The hole they needed to investigate appeared in an instant.

"Max," said McKenzie.

"I know," he said. "We have to take this stuff back when we finish."

They secured one of the ropes to a rock and dropped the bulk of it over the side. Max took the second rope over his shoulder and began to rappel down the side of the pit.

CHAPTER 22

About halfway down, he realized what he was doing. He was actually rappelling into a cave shaft somewhere in Israel. He knew, also, that he was doing something in which he had no experience or knowledge, yet the rappelling felt as normal as if he'd been doing it for years.

His flashlight showed that he was reaching the bottom of the shaft, and he slowed until his feet struck the ground. "Okay, Kenz," he yelled up to her.

In a few moments his sister stood next to him. She looked up and saw how far down they'd come. "We came down that?" she said, her eyes wide with amazement at what she had just accomplished.

"Yeah, I guess so," he mumbled. "I just knew what to do."

"So did I," she said. They stared at one another for a few moments. "We've never done any mountain climbing, have we?"

"Certainly not that I remember," he shrugged. "It looks like we were given the grace to do it. Now I know what that means."

"Yep, pretty amazing, huh?" she nodded. "Now what?"

They looked around the room. "Do you see a door or anything?" she asked.

Max walked to the wall they'd descended. Then he paused, staring. "Kenz?" he said. His sister came over.

"What's up?" she asked.

"Well, look at the pile of stones here," he said. "They aren't piled like this anywhere else."

"That's true," she agreed. "How about if we shift some of these." They set out together to move the rocks, which varied in size from basketballs on down to pebbles. It was hard and tiring work. After about a half hour, they became aware of a slight breeze coming through at the top of the pile.

"There must be a room back there," said McKenzie. "It probably has some sort of crack going outside so that fresh air can come in."

After another half hour, they had moved a lot of rock, but exhaustion was setting in. It was clear that they needed a lot more time. Max casually placed his hands in his pockets and pulled out a water bottle and a couple of snack bars. "Hey, Kenz, check your pockets!" he exclaimed.

She realized, she too, had the same items in her pockets. "All I can say is that Curiel thinks of everything. It is certainly an advantage to have him as a friend!"

They both laughed and sat for a few minutes to enjoy their snacks and renew their energy. As soon as they were finished they heard a deep, echoing voice, "use your amulets."

"Did you say that?" asked the twins in unison.

"No, Beloved," said the voice. They recognized it.

Curiel stood with them. They were so glad to see him they laughed, and McKenzie got tears in her eyes. "Dear Curiel," she said. "Have you always been here?"

"I have never left you," he said. "But hold up the amulets and let them lead you."

"Why do we keep needing to be reminded to do that?" asked Max. "We must be very slow learners." They all smiled at the comment.

Max took McKenzie's hand and again they allowed the

amulet to guide their direction. They turned to the pile of rocks, and in a moment a path appeared. Curiel just gave them a knowing glance.

"Beloved," said Curiel. "Do not let the amulets down or waver. Walk with courage. Can you do that?" The twins nodded and set out.

They walked single file down the path through the rocks. Rubble had filled the tunnel a great deal farther than they had thought. "Goodness," said McKenzie, "we would have been moving rock for days."

"Right," said Max. "But I don't think we would have lasted that long."

"Can that be the end of the path?" McKenzie asked. She glimpsed a slice of light about ten yards ahead.

"Yes, Beloved," said the voice.

In a few seconds they stepped out from the tunnel the amulets had created. They found themselves in a large chamber, perhaps thirty feet square. The room was illuminated by a soft golden glow. As they looked, they saw four large and terrifying creatures each standing in a corner of the room. The creatures were the source of the light, which reflected off many objects which had been set reverently in the center of the room.

The twins reached for Curiel. "Curiel," murmured Max, barely able to speak. Each creature had a human form but different faces: one with the head of a lion, one an ox, one an eagle, and one a man. All had six wings with eyes all around, even beneath their wings. They could see everywhere at once.

"Do not be afraid," said Curiel softly. "They are called seraphim and are guarding the great treasure lying here."

"Lo-lo-look, in the center of the room," Max pointed, his

stammering returning for the moment.

"The Ark of the Covenant," exclaimed McKenzie. "This is where it's been for nearly 3000 years, isn't it."

"Yes, Beloved," said their friend. "The Priests, under the direction of the great prophet Jeremiah, brought it here. Do not touch it yet," he cautioned. "But go and look at the Mercy seat."

Max and McKenzie knew what he meant. They walked forward, a bit leery of the guardian creatures, but the beings did not move. Still, the twins had the strong sense that the creatures were watching them intently, scrutinizing their every move. "Are you sure we are safe from uh, those beings?" Max asked Curiel in a whisper, afraid of his words echoing around the room.

"You have never been so safe in your lives," said the Angel. "Look at your passageway." The twins turned and looked. The Tunnel was again sealed with rocks.

"Oh!" said McKenzie. "No one can get in here without the amulets, can they?"

"Soon they will come and dig into this room," said Curiel. "They will do so, though, because of your exploration today. But no one will disturb you at the moment."

The twins stepped onto the platform on which the Ark stood. Being careful not to touch it, they peered at the top and saw several dark brown stains, like those they had seen on the rock underneath Calvary.

"Blood, correct?" asked Max.

"Indeed," smiled their friend, and they saw him kneeling beside the Ark.

"Can we open it?" asked McKenzie, gesturing to the top of the Ark.

"I'm afraid not," smiled their friend. "Perhaps you will be a guest when the new Levites do open it, however."

For the next several minutes, the twins explored the room. Curiel directed them to several huge piles of gold coins which were stacked around the wealth.

"What are the coins?" asked Max.

"It is the wealth of the temple at the time of Jeremiah," their friend said. "Jeremiah knew that the invaders would steal everything that was gold, and they hid the wealth of the temple here."

"Moving everything here really was an enormous amount of work," said McKenzie.

"Yes," said Curiel. "That is why Marina and Dan were so exhausted. They helped move everything. "Look," he directed. "Here is the candlestick they brought down here."

"Something occurred to me," said Max. "Are we going to forget all this?"

"I fear so, but only after a while," said their friend. "It will be necessary to protect you so you will be unable to reveal this location to anyone. You will, however, be able to remember what you have done long enough to tell the High Priest and the Prime Minister what you have seen. They will take over the recovery of these treasures at the proper time."

Now they understood. "Can we tell people what we have seen?" said Max.

"Not the general public," said Curiel. "Your families, of course, can know what you have seen. Keep this adventure secret until the temple is consecrated. It is possible that will occur in your lifetime," he added with a smile.

"Are we allowed to take anything out of here?" asked Max.

"I believe," said Curiel, "that each of you may take eight golden coins. As you can imagine, these will be heirlooms in your families. Each of you may keep one. Give one to Dan and Marina as well one to Colby and Gina with the same instructions. The rest you will give to the future high priest of Israel as evidence of your expedition."

Each twin took their coins and placed them in their pockets, keeping their eyes peeled on the creatures guarding the Ark as they did so. "Come," said Curiel. He walked with them over to the seraphim. A few of the creature's eyes followed them as they approached. The angel spoke to the creature, and they had a sense of the creature relaxing a bit. They mentioned this to Curiel.

"Yes," said Curiel. "They will not harm you. However, if you were not with me, I am afraid you would have been dead for several minutes already."

"I guess it's a good thing you showed up when you did," said Kenzie, breathing a sigh of relief.

"Will other people be safe when they come to recover the treasure then?" asked Max.

"Yes," said Curiel. "They will be temple priests consecrated to the task of recovery."

"How can we be safe?" said McKenzie. "We aren't priests. We aren't even Jewish."

"That is true," said Curiel. "However, you are safe because of what you found on the rock and on the Mercy seat. Also, and most important, because of a covenant you entered into in your Sunday School a few years ago. That is going to keep you safe for the rest of eternity."

"Oh!" said the Twins in unison. They got it.

Curiel nodded. "That, and of course, they know who sent me."

"Are you ready to go back?" asked Curiel. "It has always been appropriate to stay in the presence of the Ark for no more that just a few moments." The twins felt at the pockets of their jeans, and made sure the coins were there. They were heavy, much more so than the dimes and quarters they carried in America.

"Can we please touch the Ark before we go?" said McKenzie, sounding like she was pleading. "Maybe take a picture with our cell phones?"

"Yes, touch the Ark for a few moments," said Curiel. "Remember this moment for the rest of your lives."

The twins took pictures with their cell phones of each of them next to the Ark, as well as several other pictures of them posing with the statues of the Cherubim located on top of the Ark, the large candlesticks, the Altar of Incense, and the other treasures. Both of them were overwhelmed by the importance of their mission. They were the first humans to look at the great treasures of Israel in more than 30 centuries, and the honor of the occasion stirred them in the depth of their souls.

"Come, Beloved," said Curiel. "Well done."

In the next moment they stood in the chamber where they had found the blood on the rock. Without saying too much, they coiled up the ropes, and took off the climbing belts. Then, still silent, they used the amulets to step into the storage garage where they had borrowed the ropes and belts. They hung the ropes and the other gear where they had found it.

When everything had been returned to its proper place, they held up their amulets and returned home.

CHAPTER 23

Two weeks later, Gina and Colby called and asked if they could take the twins to dinner. Never one to turn down a free meal, Max accepted for both of them and then informed Kenzie of the date he had made. "Hey, what if I had some glamorous plans already?" she replied, kidding him.

At 7:00 P.M., they found themselves at a favorite Geneva restaurant, Riganato's, which specialized in Italian food as well as steaks and chops. The restaurant was quiet that evening and they selected a table on the porch away from other diners so they could talk about the implications of the expedition with confidentiality.

As they sat enjoying sodas, Gina insisted that they order the rib eye steaks and french fries. She ordered their stuffed red pepper appetizer and a large roasted beet salad, her favorite, for them to share.

When the waitress retreated with their orders, Gina and Colby leaned forward to hear the story of their expedition. The twins told them the narrative with as much detail as they could.

"Where are the gold coins now?" asked Gina.

"Mom and Dad took us to place them in the bank's vault," said Max.

"Yeah," said McKenzie. "We put them in safe deposit boxes."

"But we did keep some of them out," explained Max. Max dug into his pocket and handed one of the coins to his sister and one to his brother-in-law. The married couple put their heads together to examine the coins, in awe of the idea of holding history in their hands.

Gina and Colby sat back. Gina chewed her lip. "We have to keep this secret as of now, right?"

"Yes," said McKenzie. "Curiel told us to keep it very quiet."

"Why's that?" asked Colby. "Are you in danger?"

"Well, yes, we could be," said McKenzie. "One thing we found out is that there is a lot of hostility about who the Temple Mount really belongs to."

"Yeah," said Max. He flipped open his notebook and turned to a particular page. "For example, in 2003, some workmen on Temple mount found a stone inscribed with the name of King Josiah, who was King in about the seventh century B. C. Josiah became king of Judah at the age of eight."

"That was pretty young," said Colby.

"Yes," explained McKenzie. "We also found out that he was assassinated. Anyhow, the stone's inscription was authentic ancient Hebrew, and the Palestinian workers tried to destroy it, since it would give some proof that the Hebrews were on Temple Mount for centuries before the Romans expelled them from the Holy Land in 70 A. D."

Gina looked at Colby, and they both grinned. "You guys have been doing some homework," said their sister, smiling with pride at the knowledge the twins had accumulated.

"I guess so," said Max. "But we have to finish telling you what we did." For the next several moments, Max and McKenzie related their adventure in the cave under the mount of Calvary.

"You saw the actual blood of Jesus?" said Colby, his mouth hanging open.

"Right," said Gina. "Oh, boy. What now?"

"Well, we're going to go to Israel," McKenzie announced. "Marina is arranging for us to meet with her friend Stephen Levin, who has moved there. She promised to introduce us. He's quite knowledgeable about the rebuilding of the Temple. We are hoping he can get us in to talk to the Prime Minister and the Chief Rabbi."

His sister and her husband looked back and forth at one another. "Can we come?" Asked Colby.

CHAPTER 24

During summer break, the Rizza clan and their spouses boarded an El Al jet in New York for the flight to Tel Aviv. After touring the ancient land of Israel for a few days they arrived in the ancient Capital city of Jerusalem.

Marina stopped in front of an office building not far from the site of the ancient temple. "Stay here," she said. "I'll phone you when I get inside."

* * * * *

Stephen Levin sat in his office, excited at the prospect of seeing two of his very best friends from his high school days in Geneva, Illinois, that were due any minute.

He had enjoyed a rewarding experience at college. After graduation he'd come to Israel bearing two treasures of the ancient people of Israel: an almond-wood staff that had been owned by Moses himself, and the red stone known as the Urim and Thummin. He smiled to himself as he recalled the circumstances allowing him to recover the treasured items. He'd put them into the Vault of Antiquities not far from Temple Mount.

Stephen had gone into training to become a priest when he arrived in Jerusalem. He'd been polishing up his Hebrew, and studying the office of the High Priest. He would assume that title someday, when the Israelis re-built the temple in its ancient spot where the great king David had set it.

Stephen's secretary knocked and entered. "Marina and Dan are here," she announced, and stood aside as they came into the office. Stephen came around his desk and hugged his two friends and showed them to a sofa. In a few moments, he sent one of the police to fetch the rest of the family.

After several moments of conversation, Marina drew his attention to the twins who sat somewhat in awe of the situation. They were sitting in the presence of the man who, at some time, maybe in the near future, would take his place in the rebuilt temple as the hereditary office of the High Priest of Israel.

"What's up, you two?" he said, welcoming them.

"Well," said McKenzie. "We want to show you something."

They opened a small suitcase and withdrew a half a dozen gold coins and laid them on the coffee table.

Stephen sat stunned. "Where did you get these things?" he stammered.

"We know where the Ark is, too," said Max. "We can tell you, but we can't go there again."

They laid out the story of the search, the rappelling below the mount of Calvary, and the path through the debris. "The items are in pieces in the chamber," said McKenzie, as she showed him the pictures they had taken in the chamber. "It'll take a lot of effort to get them out. In addition, there are guards around the items in the chamber." With hesitation in her voice, she explained about the huge angelic creatures called *Seraphim* stationed at the four corners of the treasure chamber and described the unique appearance of each one. "I know you probably think that sounds kind of crazy, but.."

"No, that does not surprise me. But that the seraphim allowed you entrance is truly remarkable," said Stephen.

"Yes," said Max. "I am sure we were allowed because the Angel took us there. I think you will have to be the one to go in first."

Stephen sat for the next hour, listening to the twins lay out the entire story of their adventure.

"Well," he said at last. "Why can't you come along? You know, be our guide?"

"We used these items the Angel Curiel gave us. They allowed us to travel through time and space in order to complete the tasks we were given," explained McKenzie. She pulled out her amulet as Max pulled his from underneath his sweater. "But we can't use them again. They've gone dark, which tells me we have to give them away."

"You will be recovering the treasures of your nation," said Max. "We aren't citizens here."

At last Stephen Levin nodded. "We will store these items in a safe place, but we will make them available to our people to see, I think. It will give us a link to our past, but also to the One in whose honor they were consecrated."

"We agree," said the twins.

Stephen grinned at the way the twins spoke in unison. "When we again build the temple, we will of course have a ceremony of consecration."

Gina smiled at her friend. "I think you should invite the twins to the consecration, Stephen."

"That's where I was going with my comments," agreed the future High Priest. "We will have you and your family join us for the celebration and consecration, of course, as our guests."

The twins felt honored to think they would be included . "Wouldn't miss it," they replied wth a great deal of enthusiasm.

CHAPTER 25
Two months later

McKenzie and Max were sweeping out the garage, trying to get rid of a bunch of dead leaves and dirt that had accumulated since summer. "Hey, Kenz, you think we will get to go back to Disney World?" asked Max. "It seems like ages ago that we were there."

"I sure hope so. You really need a few trips to see everything. We didn't get to see all the light shows. Maybe we can plan a trip once the whole Star Wars land is completed."

"Yeah, that would be the best. I can only imagine what it will be like. From what we could glimpse of the construction site, it will be huge. Getting our picture taken with Chewbacca is a great memory, reminding us of something to look forward to. Let's bring this up at the next family dinner and try to make a plan," suggested Max. "Maybe the whole family could go together."

"Great idea!" agreed McKenzie. "And we will have to take them all to dinner at 'The Whispering Canyon Cafe."

"For sure," laughed Max. "But we can't say too much about it. We don't want to give away all the fun surprises there!"

"Agreed," said Kenzie.

The garage door was open and as they worked the radio blared out some of McKenzie's favorite music.

"Can't we listen to something else?" whined her brother.

"No!" she said, but she was smiling. "You lost the coin toss, remember?"

"I'd rather listen to a dentist's drill," he said. His sister laughed and started to retort, but a shadow fell across their cleaning project.

They looked up. "Curiel!" they said in unison.

"Hello, Beloved."

"I'm so glad to see you!" the twins exclaimed.

"And I you," he said, enfolding the twins in a hug. "I have come for the amulets, I'm afraid."

The sadness they felt at this news was evident on their faces.

"Dear young friends," said Curiel. "I am sorry. But you knew you would have to give them up sometime, didn't you?"

McKenzie and Max looked at one another. Both had tear in their eyes as they took off the medallions. Their friend took them and put them inside his cloak. Then, he hugged the twins. "Will we see you again?" asked McKenzie.

"I am never far," he replied, a twinkle in his eye. "I promise." Then, the Angel was gone.

The End

A Mouse Gate Adventure Book
What's your adventure?

www.mousegate.com

Title: *ACID*

- Author: Jeff Lovell
- Publisher: TotalRecall Publications, Inc.
- HARD COVER ISBN: 978-1-59095-116-3
- PAPERBACK, ISBN: 978-1-59095-117-0
- EBOOK, Nook, Kindle, ISBN: 978-1-59095-118-7
- Number of pages: 352
- Publication Date: 2013

Rick Howell, living in the shadow of two women who have the power to change reality, must risk his life to stop the genocidal exploits of a desperate lunatic who wants to acquire their powers. The discovery of a mind controlling drug opens a pathway to frightening mental abilities for Rachel Farrell, who can move backward and forward in time at will, while Donna Riske, Rachel's best friend, can control the thoughts of others.

Title: *The Coven of the Spring*

- Author: Jeff Lovell
- Publisher: TotalRecall Publications, Inc.
- HARD COVER ISBN: 978-1-59095-113-2
- PAPERBACK, ISBN: 978-1-59095-114-9
- EBOOK, Nook, Kindle, ISBN: 978-1-59095-115-6
- Number of pages: 336
- Publication Date: 2013

An ancient secret, with frightening new powers, emerges to terrify and destroy.

Grace DeRosa, a gifted research chemist, lives with her husband Jim and their seventeen year old daughter Crissy. Grace finds a hidden spring in the woods near Salem, Massachusetts. She discovers that the consumed water imparts unique and fearful powers that lead to the ability to read minds, create terrifying mental pictures and force the user's will on others.

Title: *Emerald*

- Author: Jeff Lovell
- Publisher: TotalRecall Publications, Inc.
- HARD COVER ISBN: 9781590950807
- PAPERBACK, ISBN: 9781590950814
- EBOOK, ISBN: 9781590950821
- Number of pages: 348
- Publication Date: 2015

Emerald begins with a pirate assault on a merchant vessel. Blackbeard, or Edward Teach, terrorized the east coast of America from Nova Scotia down to the Virgin Islands. This book shows how people with a unique mental power called the Knack fight against the evil of pirates from 1715 to the present day, and even includes a long look at the court of King Arthur, and his chief advisor Myrthynne, who also had the most powerful manifestation of the Knack. This book, then, flows in several time periods and pulls together romance, villainy and a dramatic treasure, all of which frame a love story between a woman with the Knack and a man devoted to loving and protecting her.

Title: *The Cape*

- Author: Jeff Lovell
- Publisher: TotalRecall Publications, Inc.
- HARD COVER, ISBN: 9781590952078
- PAPERBACK, ISBN: 9781590952085
- EBOOK, ISBN: 9781590952092
- Number of pages: 228
- Publication Date: 2016

People say that *Der Fleigen Hollander—The Flying Dutchman*, as it is known in English—vanished with all hands in the sixteenth century off the Cape of Good Hope. Yet the ship has been by reliable, truthful people all over the world, suggesting that the ship is trapped in a time warp somewhere in the treacherous ocean south of the Cape. When her father is kidnapped by the ship, Therese goes to find him and rescue him from the self-imposed, Purgatorial imprisonment. In the search she is joined by her mother and a lifetime best friend, who seek to help Therese draw his soul back from the pit of Hell before he is lost for all eternity.

Title: *Ghost Of White Island*

- Author: Jeff Lovell
- Publisher: TotalRecall Publications, Inc.
- HARD COVER ISBN: 9781590951194
- PAPERBACK, ISBN: 9781590952092
- EBOOK, Nook, Kindle, ISBN: 9781590952092
- Number of pages: 348
- Publication Date: 2015

In 1715, a ship's carpenter tried to rape the 14 year old daughter of the captain of a British warship and was flogged almost to death. He mutinied and captured the ship, killing the captain and forcing his daughter into marriage. After falling in with Blackbeard, he abandoned his young wife on a cold, bitter rock called White Island, off the coast of New Hampshire. When he was caught and hanged by the British Navy, his treasure vanished into history. Many people believe that Martha, his reluctant wife, hid the treasure in the Isle of Shoals chain. This is the story of a search for those gold and jewels and treasure, protected by the Ghost of White Island.

Title: *The Third Day*

- Author: Jeff Lovell
- Publisher: TotalRecall Publications, Inc.
- HARD COVER ISBN: 9781590959947
- PAPERBACK, ISBN: 9781590959954
- EBOOK, Nook, Kindle, ISBN: 9781590959961
- Number of pages: 288
- Publication Date: 2016

The Old, old man walks in all the countries of the world, tracing and retracing and tracing again his betrayal, unable to find peace or grace since his betrayal of the Nazarene some two thousand years ago. Two newlywed young people and their spouses find themselves called to help him and recover an incalculably valuable treasure, worth far more than any earthly price. The group must go to the Virgin Islands and recover the treasure to help the Old Man redeem his soul and save others from a disastrous fate at the hands of a desperate cult.

Title: *Jazz and Ella*

- Author: Jeff & Jacqi Lovell
- Publisher: TotalRecall Publications, Inc.
- PAPERBACK, ISBN: 9781590953006
- EBOOK, ISBN: 9781590953013
- Number of pages: 104
- Publication Date: 2015

Jazz and Ella tells the story of Jazz, a fourteen year old high school freshman, and his best friend, Ella, who meet on the way to Disney World. A supernatural being gives them each a magic amulet, which the children use to transport themselves to new and different worlds. They meet and deal many situations that cause them to face their fears and even terrors; that suggest ways that situations can be handled; and they see some of the choices that they will have to confront as they grow up.

Title: *Gina and Colby*

- Author: Jeff & Jacqi Lovell
- Publisher: TotalRecall Publications, Inc.
- PAPERBACK, ISBN: 9781590953259
- EBOOK, ISBN: 9781590953266
- Number of pages: 136
- Publication Date: 2016

A Magic Amulet Allows Two Teen-Agers to Discover how to Make a Difference in the World of Animal Poaching

Two teen-agers, different in every way, form an unshakeable friendship as a result of the adventures they share after meeting in Disney Springs. Transported through a magic amulet to a totally different culture and continent, they are offered an opportunity to make a difference in the lives of endangered animals.

Dangers abound as they face poachers and pirates in their attempts to rescue these creatures, and they discover a courage within themselves that leads each one to a positive change in how they view themselves and others.

Title: *Marina and Dan*

- Author: Jeff & Jacqi Lovell
- Publisher: TotalRecall Publications, Inc.
- PAPERBACK, ISBN: 9781590953228
- EBOOK, Nook, Kindle, ISBN: 9781590953242
- Number of pages: 128
- Publication Date: 2016

This ancient Egyptian Adventure, part of the Mousegate Series, traces the story of Marina and Dan, best friends since childhood, as they wrestle with the concept of heroism and how it applies to them. When offered a unique, but potentially dangerous opportunity by a spiritual being, they must make a decision that will stretch them in ways they never imagined. Able to experience first-hand the miraculous events that have been talked about for centuries, they witness the impossible become possible as they walk with Moses during the ancient biblical era where the crossing of the Red Sea took place. Both their friendship and their faith is strengthened through the adventures encountered together.

Title: *Max and McKenzie*

- Author: Jeff & Jacqi Lovell
- Publisher: TotalRecall Publications, Inc.
- PAPERBACK, ISBN: 9781590953334
- EBOOK, Nook, Kindle, ISBN: 9781590953341
- Number of pages: 150
- Publication Date: 2017

Max and McKenzie, teenaged twin brother and sister, receive magic amulets which allow them to time-travel to sites in ancient Israel. They witness Elijah's defeat of the prophets of Baal, and journey to the ancient temple of Solomon to assist in the removal of the temple treasures before the invasion of the forces of Egypt. They witness the theft of the Ark of the Covenant and its return to Israel by the Philistine forces, and march around the city of Jericho with the Israeli forces. In the climactic scene, they explore the Mount of Calvary to find the lost treasures of the temple. In their treasure hunting, they learn valuable lessons about self-confidence, personal faith, and persistent courage.

9781590953334